Steven O'Connor was born in England and migrated to Australia with his family when he was a teenager. He works at the Department of Education developing programs for schools. Steven enjoys electronic gaming and can proudly say he has beaten Halo, Bioshock and Mortal Kombat without having to stoop to the use of the easy setting. This is his first novel.

EleMental

COME TO VIRTUALITEE AND SEE FOR YOURSELF

STEVEN O'CONNOR

PIER **9**

Published in 2010 by Pier 9, an imprint of Murdoch Books Pty Limited

Murdoch Books Australia
Pier 8/9
23 Hickson Road
Millers Point NSW 2000
Phone: +61 (0) 2 8220 2000
Fax: +61 (0) 2 8220 2558
www.murdochbooks.com.au

Murdoch Books UK Limited
Erico House, 6th Floor
93–99 Upper Richmond Road
Putney, London SW15 2TG
Phone: +44 (0) 20 8785 5995
Fax: +44 (0) 20 8785 5985
www.murdochbooks.co.uk

Publisher: Colette Vella
Project Editor: Kate Fitzgerald
Editor: Ali Lavau
Designer: Hugh Ford
Illustrations: Aaron Pocock

National Library of Australia Cataloguing-in-Publication Data
Author: O'Connor, Steven
Title: EleMental : Come to Virtualitee and see for yourself/
                  Steven O'Connor
ISBN: 978-1-74196-713-5 (pbk.)
Target Audience: For young adults.
Subjects: Electronic games--Juvenile fiction.
                  Video game addiction--Juvenile fiction.
Dewey Number: A823.4

PRINTED IN AUSTRALIA

For Gina, for everything

'A gamer never leaves
a game unfinished.'

Zeb Redman, 2050

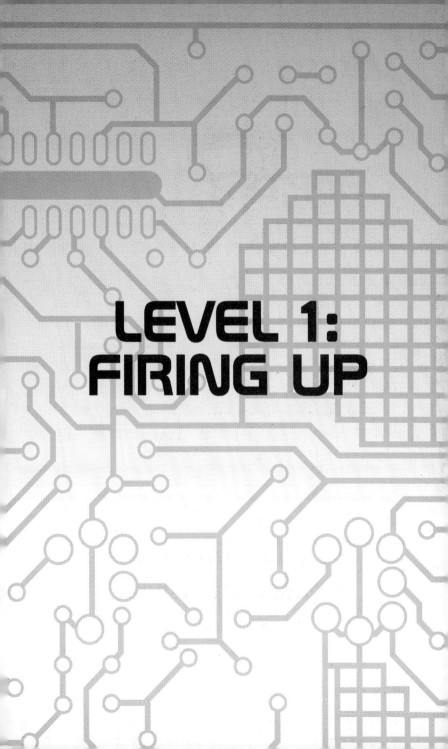

LEVEL 1:
FIRING UP

CHAPTER 1

Zeb Redman cursed as he spun around the corner, balancing on his speeding hyperboard, and saw the last thing he wanted to see. The queue at Screamers Virtual Games Universe was mammoth. It snaked from somewhere deep within the store, out through its snapping auto-doors and stretched out of sight down the street. The disappointment gnawed at him. Wagging school had made no difference.

The store's flashing signs seemed to taunt him: *Experience the new Plush. Free trials all day. Don't miss out.*

Zeb sighed, flipped from his hovering hyperboard, and landed on the street kerb. Far in front of him, perched at the head of the queue, some lucky guy was set to be the first to experience the new Plush DVP – deep virtual player – games console. Zeb gazed the other way, down the shuffling queue of hopefuls. At ten minutes a turn, it would be nighttime before his chance at a free try-out came around. The place would be closed by then.

He closed his eyes and released a slow breath, relaxing as he'd trained himself to do prior to taking on a high-level boss enemy. As in games, so in life. He decided to go in anyway. With all this commotion going on, you never knew what you might find. He worked his way through the queue and into the store. People glared, but he held up his arms, all innocence. 'It's all right. Not queue jumping. Just trying to get in.'

With the rack full, he was forced to carry his hyperboard. He wandered the aisles of expensive games that filled the store's shelves, thoughts of which monopolised his every waking moment. Especially the gleaming rows of gloss-wrapped 2050 first-person shooter new releases – games with packaging that sported moving images of exploding army death-tanks, multi-headed trolls with weapons the size of cannons, grinning aliens with scarred and bloodied bodies ... Xtreme-rated horrocore. All bearing the latest in ziptech security seals. Impossible to steal.

But his instinct for an opportunity had been right. The crowds fussing over the new games console provided an excellent diversion. After a period of frustrated browsing (everything was out of his price range!), he spied something he knew he could have – with a bit of skill and luck. An old first-person shooter called *Hoolyguns*. It was sticking out of the corner of a weightless sales bin otherwise chock-a-block with dated v'romances and offworld tour guides.

He slung his hyperboard across his back, straightened his bag at his side, and spent a good hour stalking the bin as it floated through the store's aisles. Waiting for the right moment. And as it drifted towards an out-of-the-way exit, far from the winding queue and the onlookers clustered at Plush gamespace-windows *oohing* and *aahing* at the virtual action within, Zeb's own excitement mounted. Though it wasn't Xtreme-rated or anything, it looked compatible with his old Magnum 50. So who was he to complain? He, with only a Magnum console at home and nothing decent to play on it. He, who hungered for any first-person shooter. New, old, secondhand, whatever.

And it bore an ancient security imprint. As far as Zeb was concerned, it was a giveaway and the disappointment about the Plush try-out slipped from his mind.

He watched. He crept forward. He waited.

A zipcam meandered up and stopped close to the bin. It clicked and hissed as it lowered itself to the floor, its many lenses rotating. Then it lifted again and moved on, heading down a nearby aisle.

Now! Moving in, Zeb hustled the bin up against the wall. Using his body to block the view of anyone who might be watching, he snatched the game from the sales bin, pulled a screwdriver from his pocket, squeezed it so that a sharp stick of blue laser shot out, and slash, cut, strip! Security imprint: gone.

Plunging the game into the depths of his bag, he was out that door.

Back home, Zeb hurried down the corridor towards his bedroom.

His mother shouted something from her room, her words muffled. He detected the sounds of her Zeeplayer. Stopping, he pressed an ear to her door. A spacefront reporter was in the middle of an update on the asteroid mining disputes. '*Growing even more unstable,*' the male voice said. The voice cut off and Zeb heard the strains of a drippy soap opera. His mother had flicked channels.

He pushed on down the corridor. 'Hi, Mum,' he yelled as he passed her door. 'Gotta study. Like we agreed.'

He imagined her in there: propped up on a pillow, Zeeplayer turned to maxiwidth and smothering the opposite wall in embracing arms and bodies, couples tangled together. Her glass within easy reach. If his dad weren't off spacefronting, it would be a different story. Forget it, Zeb told himself. Who needed a father? Focus on the gaming. There was nothing like it. The real world could go suck.

He booted his door shut, kicked some strewn clothes out of the way and crouched before his Magnum 50, which sat on an old plastic crate near his bed. He hit the small switch on its face and waited. When nothing happened, he slapped it. 'Wake up!' he growled.

A dull red light flickered and a square opened at the console's centre, gaping like a hungry mouth. Digging deep into his bag, he seized the game. He drew it out, removed the shiny black cube from its packaging and fed it into the console.

Jumping up, Zeb dragged his bedroom's dusty curtains closed, cutting out all light from the real world.

'Attention, Magnum,' he said. 'Seal room for sound and start game.'

Turning, he watched as the game kicked in. His messy bedroom melted away, replaced by ...

Hoolyguns
A first-person shooter
(Deleted title – pay no more than $650.00, incl. GST)

Zeb skipped the recommended pre-game training and went straight in at the first level.

Immediately, a groaning sound like the bending of steel engulfed him, and the floor shuddered as a complete street scene wrenched into existence, materialising beneath his feet and stretching out on all sides.

Zeb let his gaze wander, turning a full circle and taking it all in.

It was a bright, virtual version of a sunny day. A deserted street. Early century by the looks of things. Something like 2010 – his parents would have been kids. He squinted in the light, searching for signs of enemy activity. Nothing.

The small shape of a zipcar buzzed into view and shot on by. Zeb frowned. This game scenario was set in pre-ziptech times. They didn't have zipcars back then! Did they think all virtual gamers were kactoheads? A tram rattled past in the distance. It travelled on the ground. Well, they'd got that right.

A door banged somewhere and Zeb swung around, tracking the sound. Four zombified men clutching the necks of broken bottles staggered from a nearby pub, their blank, undead faces pasty and dry, even in the heat. Their coarse grey coveralls bore the distinctive logo of space miners – a sparking drill over a lump of spinning rock. Zeb groaned. Another mistake in the game. Asteroid mining in 2010? No way.

One of the zombie spacers noticed Zeb and pointed him out to the others, grunting and murmuring. The others murmured back. 'Urrgh, urrrgh.' They elbowed each other and staggered forwards.

'Attention, game,' Zeb shouted. 'Weapon!'

'What weapon do you choose?' said a voice in the air. It was the game voice, female, polite. The zombified spacers continued in his direction, unperturbed by the disembodied enquiry.

'I don't care – anything.'

'Confirmed.'

A pair of boxing gloves appeared, laced tightly at his wrists. Zeb stared at his hands in disbelief. 'Attention, game.' He nodded towards his opponents. 'I know I said anything, but boxing gloves against jagged beer bottles? Seems a bit mismatched. How about a dagger?' The gloves disappeared and a giant, zip-powered machine-gun appeared in his arms. 'Or a ginormous gun,' Zeb added.

He clutched it, fighting against its weight; he was barely able to keep its barrel from dragging on the ground. His fingers accidentally tightened on the trigger as he tried to level it and bullets ripped into the tarmac centimetres from his toes. At the same time, the weapon's butt recoiled into his chest, pushing him backwards.

His opponents halted.

Zeb dumped the gun to the ground. 'Attention, game. Too easy! I'd mow 'em down in a nanosecond.' It wasn't really the game's fault. His Magnum's v-graphics card was Jurassic – eLusions were only as good as your DVP. 'Game, give me something more challenging.'

'Confirmed,' said the game voice.

Zeb held out an arm and a long whip appeared in the air before his hand. He snatched at it before it fell to the ground. It crackled with blue and white sparks at its tip. Zeb grinned. 'Zoomin. This is more like it.'

Zeb eyed the words *Ammo Count: 10* that appeared in the sky above his head. Ten? Ha!

'Urrgh, urrrgh,' said the spacers, moving again.

Zeb flicked the whip. Sparks crackled down its length and it reared into the air like a battle stallion. 'Come and get me!' he cried in triumph. But he let the whip fall back to the ground. One weak blue spark dripped from it before it lay still. The ammo count changed to 9. Zeb glanced at it, then stared at the whip and up at the spacers. He slowly backed away.

The spacers, looking enthused, raised their arms as they drew close. Almost upon him, their zombie murmuring grew in intensity.

Smiling, Zeb raised the whip and lashed out once more. This time it cracked loudly and the air sizzled as the whip cut through it. A small electric storm discharged from its sparking length and streaked at them. The first spacer took the brunt of the shock and stood stock still, electric bolts of changing colour running through him. He fell backwards, rigid, connecting with the others, and the bolt ran through them all. They collapsed into a muddled heap and lay there. The ammo count flicked to 8.

'Score,' said the game voice. 'Zeb Redman: twenty; space miners: zero.'

Zeb surveyed the scene, waiting and hoping for better combat.

A heavy scraping sound broke the silence, and a short distance away, a manhole cover pushed up and sideways. Zeb watched as long white fingers appeared from beneath it. A rich, moist smell snaked into the air. He tensed, his whip poised. Rake-thin creatures, wet and grey, like eels with elongated limbs, scrambled from the dark hole. Four, five, six, they stood hunched and held their bony arms out towards Zeb.

Zeb watched, unimpressed, hands on his hips. Was that it?

With a flick of their wrists, things changed. Each of the creatures' arms now ended in a fistful of bristling needles. One flicked his wrist again, and a long needle streaked from it. Zeb leapt to one side as it spiralled *hooly, hooly, hooly* past his ear.

'So you're the Hoolyguns, eh?' Zeb said to himself. He sucked in a deep breath. 'Attention, game,' he cried with delight. 'Shield!' He held out an arm in readiness.

'Confirmed,' said the game voice.

A shield, long and brilliant white, appeared and Zeb grabbed it. In the same instant, an ice blue *Defence* bar meter materialised below the ammo count. Zeb grasped the whip firmly, and shifted himself sideways behind the shield as the Hoolyguns circled him, flicking their wrists and sending needles spinning at him. Zeb dodged, blocked, rolled and ducked, lifting and twirling the shield as if it was a natural extension of himself. The gyrating needles whistled *hooly hooly hooly* past him or shattered into splinters against his shield. He glanced up at the defence meter, now half drained of colour.

The Hoolyguns hissed in frustration.

More scrambled from the manhole to join them. There were now fifteen and they tightened their circle, hunching down and shuffling from side to side, reminding Zeb of a cross between orangutans and a line of clog dancers.

But something else also happened. Further down the road a bed appeared. Zeb recognised it: the messed-up sheets, the graffiti scratched into the wood. It was his bed.

The Hoolyguns turned and saw it too. They pointed at it, shook their heads and shrugged at each other.

Then Zeb's heavy studistation materialised on top of the muddle of defeated space miners, flattening them further into the ground.

'Oh what!' Zeb cried.

At the sound of his angry voice, the Hoolyguns turned back towards him. Spitting and wheezing, they approached again.

'Oh, come on,' said Zeb. 'You're going to keep playing? There's my bed over there! Realspace is leaking in everywhere.'

The Hoolyguns took another look at the bedroom furniture, shrugged again, then hunched back into fighting positions.

But Zeb had had enough. 'Attention, game, you can forget it, I'm shutting down.'

'Confirmed,' said the game voice.

'Thanks for trying. It's not your fault. Attention, Magnum, you piece of garbage, shut down the game. And yourself too, while you're about it.' He hurled his shield at the nearest Hoolygun.

It threw up a skinny arm but had clearly not been expecting the manoeuvre and toppled over backwards.

The street trembled and began to retract, tugging at further surroundings. Whole buildings collapsed inwards with a crash of bricks and a shattering of glass, whomping thick dust into the air. Structures everywhere folded, rolling up like rugs and exposing beneath them the walls and floor of Zeb's bedroom. The Hoolyguns coughed in the dust, horror widening their eyes. One after the other, the Magnum's shutdown program whipped them off their feet and dragged them spinning into its folding. Bricks, bitumen, flattened space miners, frightened Hoolyguns, all spun into a tight, bright spot of light and hung there, at the centre of Zeb's room. Then – *pop!* – the spot disappeared.

Zeb marched over to the Magnum 50 and raised an angry foot. He wanted to kick it hard. He wanted to feel it crumble and smash under his feet. He wanted to dance on it until there was nothing but shattered pieces crushed into the floor. But what would he do after that?

He let his foot drop.

Sighing, he went in search of a tool kit.

CHAPTER 2

When Willis Jaxon woke, he felt something at the bottom of his bed. It pressed into his toes. He sat up and peered at a large gift-wrapped box. Pushing back his blankets, he shifted towards it and entered his family password into the black security seal that protruded from one corner. The packaging accepted the code with a quiet *blip* and the panels folded down and shrivelled away, leaving a sleek white machine on the bed before him. A Plush DVP console. Willis stared at it in confusion. The curved front glowed dimly, as if waiting to blink into life and greet him. He leant forward, over its smooth, flat top and peered down. Its back sprouted myriad tiny plugs as fine as caterpillar fur, its zippatronic configurations.

There was a sound by the door and Willis glanced up into his mother's watching eyes. He hadn't noticed her enter the room.

'Happy birthday, son,' she said. 'Do you like it?'

'A Plush?'

She beamed. 'Welcome to the zippy generation.'

Willis laughed. 'It's *zipgen*. Thanks, Mum.'

'And Dad,' she added. 'His big redundancy package helped pay for it.'

Willis said, 'I'll be sure to thank him – if he ever comes out of that new home office of his.' He returned his gaze to the Plush. 'No one, but *no one*, has one of these.'

'And the study games are more entertaining than they used to be,' his mother said. 'That's what the salesman said anyway. You should invite one of your classmates over to check it out with you.'

Willis didn't answer. Instead he grabbed his Zeepad from the bedside table and waved it over the Plush. The Zeepad blipped and he peered intently at the instructions now scrolling across its illuminated face. But he couldn't concentrate on the words; he knew his mum was still watching him. It felt like a too-hot sun burning his skin. He sighed, giving in, and looked up at her. 'Mum, I've barely been there a month.'

'Time enough to make some friends, surely?'

'I don't want any friends,' Willis lied. He waved a hand at the console before him and grimaced. 'Though I could do with someone to help me with this.'

His mother smiled. 'Good.'

The Zeepad chose that moment to chirp and throw up a personalised holo-ad. The image of a tiny grey figure in a long black overcoat and sunglasses gyrated a few centimetres above the Zeepad screen. The figure looked fuzzy, as if slightly out of focus. *'Happy birthday, you lucky Plush owner, you,'* it peeped. *'Come to Virtualitee ...'* – it hung on to the last syllable of *Virtualitee* for seconds: *teeeeeeeee* – *'... and get what's owing ye!'* *Yeeeeeeeeee.*

Then tinny trumpets squealed, followed by a jingle: *'Come to Virtualiteeee and see for yourself, yip, yip, yippeeee! I'm virtually yours – you're virtually mine!'* The last words were spoken in a mock-seductive manner.

Willis and his mother were both laughing as Willis switched his Zeepad off. He felt relieved by the interruption, as silly as the holo-ad had been.

Later, his mum called Willis from his room for his birthday breakfast. He strolled into the kitchen just in time to see her yank at a ring-pull sticking from the end of a flashmeal packet. He smiled in appreciation; he knew how much she hated the things. And she'd bought a full hot breakfast: the muddle of bacon, fried eggs, hash browns and baked beans popped and crackled as she poured it from the sparking packet and onto a waiting plate. Steam rose from it as it completed its self-cook program.

His dad entered the kitchen, holding his glasses in one hand and rubbing at his eyes. Willis thanked him for the Plush.

His dad seemed pleased. 'You're very welcome. Just don't ask me to help set it up! I'm liable to break it.'

Willis sat down at the table as his dad sidled up to his mum and kissed her. Not a peck on the cheek either – a lingering kiss on the lips. His mum wriggled away but her face glowed.

Willis screwed up his face in distaste. 'Dad,' he muttered, 'not in front of the children.'

His dad chuckled. 'Sorry, son, but I just can't help myself. She's one gorgeous chickadee.'

Willis mimicked a gag reflex. He was glad that his parents were so happy these days. His dad was like a new person since he'd left his stressful job and started his own business. Still, Willis wished he'd tone it down a bit.

His dad stretched an arm around his mum's waist. 'And besides, there's something else we should acknowledge while we're celebrating.'

Willis leant forward. 'Oh? And what's that?'

'Not today,' his mum said. 'This is Willis's day. Let's just celeb—'

'Your mum's only gone and done it,' his dad jumped in. 'She's got her permit.'

Willis was intrigued. 'Permit? For what?'

His mum smiled. 'I found the good news on my Zeepad late last night.' She swivelled her arms in the air as if driving a vehicle. Willis stared at her trying to read her thoughts. His dad beamed at her. Then a thought struck Willis. What was that she'd said a few weeks ago and he'd instantly dismissed as stupid and never likely to happen? 'This hasn't got anything to do with zipcars, has it?'

'Yes!' she said with glee. 'Now that we're at last settled in the one place, I have found my very own job, doing something I've always wanted to do: I'm going to be a zipcar instructor.'

Willis couldn't imagine doing anything worse – or more dangerous. But he slowly nodded at his proud parents. 'That's ... wonderful.' It seemed that everyone was happy in their new home – except him.

The ziptram swung around a group of slower-moving zipcars, hurtled towards the tram stop and slammed to the ground. Willis shoved the safety bar from him, and as it rose towards the ceiling with a hiss he grabbed hold of his hyperboard. It was one of the small ziptrams with everyone packed in tight. He worked around a mumbling, half-unconscious man, accidentally treading on his foot. The man yelped then returned to his murmuring. The real show was inside his head, Willis thought as he clambered down the tram's steps.

Students milled about the school gates. As Willis stepped through, he paused the obligatory moment to ensure the security beam detected him for the attendance register. At the same moment, tinny trumpets squealed from his school bag. He groaned and moved aside to let other students pass. They paid him no attention as he threw his bag to the ground, crouched and rummaged through it. When he produced his Zeepad, the tiny figure he'd seen on the holo-ad earlier that morning jigged up and down over the screen.

'Happy birthday, you lucky Plush owner, you!' it peeped. *'Now come to Virtualitee and get what's owing ye! Yip yip yippee!'*

The head of one passing student snapped around at the sound. He stopped and watched with amusement as Willis shut the holo-ad off.

'Everything okay?' the student asked.

Willis eyed him suspiciously. He wore the latest in hyperboard gear: a short jacket, skin-thin gloves, moulded black jeans, squared kneepads and wide sucker runners. He was tall and would stand out anywhere. But, more than that, he had presence and style – he was the last student Willis would have expected to stop and talk to him.

Willis grimaced. 'I thought these promo things were only meant to cut in on your Zeepad the once.'

'They are.'

'This one's been going off all morning. And always with the same hideous little man.'

The student looked amused. 'I'm Zeb, by the way.'

Willis nodded, amazed he still hadn't moved on.

'And you are?' Zeb asked.

'You want to know my name?' Willis was puzzled. 'Willis,' he said.

'Good to meet you, Willis. Man of the moment.' Zeb beamed at him.

'I'm sorry, *man of the moment*?'

'Who else in this rathole owns a Plush console?'

'I only got it this morning. How on earth did you know?'

'Your holo-ad was just singing about it.'

'Ah, I didn't realise you heard all that.'

'Every last syllable.'

Willis was aware he sounded nervous. They'd just met, yet Zeb spoke so easily, without the slightest trace of self-consciousness. How did he do that? Willis shoved his Zeepad into his bag and stood up. Zeb was a full head taller than him. And now that he was closer, he noticed Zeb's eyes. Full of energy. His gaze felt intense. It didn't matter that a scrap of blond hair partly covered one eye.

Willis lowered his gaze. 'You're welcome to come over and check it out,' he mumbled. 'We don't have to be full-on gamemates or anything,' he added, feeling foolish. 'But we could game a bit together.'

Zeb grinned. 'Zoomin!' he said. 'When, birthday boy?'

Willis swallowed. 'Dunno. I …' His mother had suggested this very thing that morning, but he'd never imagined it might happen. He'd not dreamt of asking her *when*.

'Tonight?' Zeb asked.

'*Tonight?*'

Zeb gave him a broad, winning smile. 'Sure.'

Willis's mother opened the door before he even reached it. 'How was school today? Better?'

Willis grimaced and inclined his head backwards with a slight roll of his eyes. He saw her take in Zeb's presence behind him. A look of delight sprang to her face.

'Well, hello,' she gushed.

Willis cleared his throat. 'Mum, this is Zeb Redman. From school.'

Zeb nodded.

'He's into gaming. That's why he's here. Come to check out my Plush.'

'A friend!' She stood back, ushering Zeb in. 'Come in, come in!'

Willis felt nauseous. 'I said he was just here to check out the Plush.'

As if things weren't bad enough, Willis's dad appeared behind his mum. Once – when his dad still had his old job – Willis saw little of him. Now he seemed to be everywhere. It was good, really. But sometimes you could have too much of a good thing.

'Hello,' his dad said. 'Any friend of Willis is a friend of ours. Come in!'

Zeb smirked at Willis as he stepped past him through the door to stand alongside Willis's parents. Willis hurried after him and led Zeb down the corridor to his bedroom.

'Perhaps you and your new friend would like some

leftover birthday cake?' his mum called after them. 'In case you get hungry? While you're gaming?'

'Shut up,' Willis hissed quietly between clenched teeth.

'They go on a bit. Your parents,' Zeb said, kicking Willis's bedroom door closed and throwing his hyperboard and bag on the floor. He peered about the room. 'So where is it, then?'

Willis wasn't sure why, but he felt reluctant to answer straight away. 'I s'pose you're wondering why they're making such a big deal of your visit,' he said instead.

Zeb shrugged and plopped down on Willis's bed. He stretched out, placing his hands behind his head. 'Nope.'

'Dad used to be in security. But he got a big payout and has started up his own consultancy thing. We used to be on the road all the time, going from town to town, wherever he was needed, so I never really had a chance to make friends. This is the first time we've had a proper home.'

'Uh-huh.'

Willis yanked the curtains closed. The bedroom light sprang on in response. When he turned back, Zeb was up on his feet and peering around the room again.

'What about you?' Willis asked. 'Are your parents as embarrassing as mine?'

Zeb looked uncomfortable. 'Dad's offworld,' he said eventually. 'We need the money bad.'

'Mars Station?'

'No, spacefronting. The asteroid mines, to be exact. He thought it was just going to be Mars Station but he was wrong. I suppose they tell everybody that until they get them up there. Lousy Space Guard.'

Willis couldn't keep the shock from his face.

'It's not as bad up there as everyone makes out,' Zeb continued. 'And it's only temporary. He'll be back any day now. Probably.' Zeb sighed. 'Look, just show me the Plush, will you?'

Willis headed over to a wooden stool against the wall. 'Under here. For safe-keeping.' He lifted up the stool to reveal the console. As if in greeting, its tiny lights blinked at them.

Zeb hurried over and knelt before it as if it was an altar. 'It's beeeeauuuutiful.'

'And there's no sound leakage whatsoever. No matter how high the volume.'

'Who helped you set it up?'

Willis smiled. 'No one.'

Zeb examined it closely. 'So d'you know how it works?' When Willis paused, Zeb looked up at him.

'What console did you graduate from?'

'This is my first.'

'Your first!' He shook his head. 'Hell. You've gone straight in at the top.'

Willis's smile stretched. 'I guess I have,' he said. 'What kind of console do you have?'

Zeb waved a hand. 'Forget it. You don't want to know. You've no idea what you've got here, have you? This thing doesn't just smother you with virtual images; it recycles them through your mind, pushing on senses you didn't even know you had.' He bent down to examine it again. 'The trick is to surrender to it. Well, show us what you've got. I can't wait to game up.'

Willis pointed to his small collection. Three. They sat neatly on his desk between two bookends. Jumping up, Zeb flicked through the flat cases: *Staying Slim in Space: Female Astronauts Tell Their Secrets*; *Star-yachting – Around the Moon in 0.00833 (repeating) Lunar Days*; and *Home Cooking the Martian Way*.

Zeb's brow furrowed. 'You've gotta be kidding.'

'They came with the Plush.'

'I was worried you mightn't have a first-person shooter, but these aren't even games.'

'I haven't had a chance to get any yet.'

'So what was your mum going on about when she said *gaming*?'

Willis shrugged.

Zeb closed his eyes for a moment, then opened them. 'Okay, this is what we do. It's too late now, but tomorrow we'll hunt out that place in the holo-ad. Collect on that offer. Play the ad again. Let's see it.'

'Oh. I deleted it.'

Zeb groaned. 'That was an exclusive offer.'

'That little guy in the overcoat and shades creeped me out.'

'All right, plan B. Did you get any birthday money? You must have, a kid like you. Tomorrow, we go to Screamers.'

'Okay, I'll let Mum know I'll be late home.'

Zeb stretched out on Willis's bed and yawned, hands behind his head. 'No need. I'm not suggesting we go after school.'

It took a moment for Zeb's comment to register. 'You mean *instead* of school?'

Zeb grinned one of his winning grins.

CHAPTER 3

Willis's stomach tightened in nervousness. And as much as he tried to hide his unease, he knew Zeb could tell. They sat on a patch of ground behind the disused school labs – a security blank spot, invisible to roving zipcams and eavesdropping devices.

'Right,' Zeb said, standing. 'Enough talking. Let's go.' As Willis climbed to his feet, Zeb patted him on the arm. 'It's really not that hard.'

They strapped their bags securely across their shoulders, picked up their hyperboards, and turned to face the school. Willis's legs shook as they approached. At the gates, he held his hyperboard tightly. They walked a few steps behind everyone else and paused as the beam hit them, letting the Automated School Security System get a long, clear shot. In the event they were reported AWOL, the ASSS record would show beyond a doubt they'd entered the school premises. That was the plan anyway, and Zeb swore by it.

'Not a word,' Zeb whispered as they crossed the threshold of the school's main building.

They scooted down a corridor and ducked into the female toilets – risky, but the only blank spot in the building that also possessed a window at the other end. Zeb seemed to know about them all. Zeb kept his back flat to the wall, directly beneath a camera. When he reached the long metal sink opposite the cubicle doors, he dropped and crawled along the floor underneath it. Willis followed more awkwardly, inching his hyper-slukboard along with him.

Then they heard a female voice from behind a closed cubicle door. 'Is someone there?' it whispered.

They moved quickly. Beyond the sink was an odd little alcove with a small window. It was easy to see why it was a blank spot. They slunk from under the sink and into the alcove, pushed the window open, shoved their hyperboards out and climbed through. It was quite a drop to the street below and Willis felt his bones shudder as he landed and crouched next to Zeb.

Willis put his lips to Zeb's ear. 'Someone heard us.'

Zeb smirked. 'Yeah, I recognised the voice. Arizona.'

Willis nodded. She was in their year.

'Hang on.' Zeb clambered back up to the window ledge and eased the window open. 'Seeyalater, Arizona!' he shouted, pitching his voice high to fool the ASSS.

The window fell back with a clatter as he jumped down and they ran off. Glancing back, Willis saw the window opening again. Turning, he concentrated on running faster. He stretched his legs until they ached, hoping to be out of sight before anyone could spot them.

Zeb came to a halt a street away from the school and stood gasping, waiting for Willis to catch up.

'Do you think she knew it was you?' Willis panted.

'Who cares? Arizona's no snitch.'

It took them thirty minutes to get to Screamers, Zeb cutting corners like there was no tomorrow, his board's suspension lasers – fixed to the sides – spinning fast. Willis could barely keep up. Turning the last bend, he saw Zeb leap from his board, kick it back and catch it as it flipped in the air. He ran into the store without checking to see if Willis was still with him.

Signs blazed across the store's windows: *Screamers!!! The louder your screams, the happier we are. We're a total scream.*

Willis thought better of kicking his hyperboard back. Stepping down, he picked it up, and followed Zeb inside.

The door spoke cheerfully as he crossed the threshold. 'Welcome to your one-stop scream shop – for all your screaming needs.'

Willis dropped his hyperboard in the rack, next to Zeb's, taking the last available slot. A bargain bin drifted in his direction and he edged past it as he headed down the nearest aisle, searching for Zeb. He found him deep within the store, ensconced in a generic gamespace booth, trialling a game. Willis stepped back from the booth and read the words that hung in the air over it: *Catapult yourself into shooter fun with* Cat Zap Zombies.

Willis ducked his head back in. Zeb stood in the centre of an arena swinging a cat by the tail in wide arcs above his head. The cat wriggled and small electrical discharges spat and popped from its whiskers. An assortment of zombies dressed as teachers, doctors and nurses surrounded him, pressing in on him.

Zeb's gaze rested on Willis. 'Look around,' he said, his circular momentum with the cat not wavering in the slightest. 'I'll catch up with you when I've found something worth getting.'

Willis gazed around the arena in awe. 'How about this? It looks amazing!'

Zeb let the cat fly. *Zyeeeooooww.* It streaked towards a zombie doctor brandishing a long scalpel, knocking him down in a crescendo of sparks. The other zombies fell back, frightened.

Zeb stared at Willis, his face appalled. 'This is just old stuff jacked up to be Plush compatible. Take my word for it, we can do a lot better than this.'

Willis did as he was told and wandered around the store. At the very back of the giant space, he found a dilapidated v'stage. He'd never seen one before – they predated even the earliest of DVPs. You had to do your virtual gaming on the stage. Some of the thick cables that hung from the rafters were still active, shifting slightly. When Willis moved closer, fascinated, several cables jerked, hissing and coiling like preying snakes.

Willis backed away.

A monitor screen fixed to the end of a mechanical arm whirled in close to him, stopping mere centimetres from his nose. A man's luminescent face glared from the screen.

'You intend to play or what?' the face asked.

Willis shook his head.

'Then move on.'

Willis did. Other customers shuffled around, avoiding eye contact with each other. They shopped alone. No pairs, no groups. Steering clear of a trembling, hunched-over man staring intently at the rows of games, Willis stumbled into another doing the same. The man elbow-shoved Willis face-first into the opposite shelf and lumbered on as games clattered to the floor.

'Push 'em back!' Zeb shouted from somewhere.

Willis looked around until he found him. Zeb now sat on the floor at the end of the aisle, a crooked stack of games between his legs.

'Don't let dirty gamefreaks walk all over you,' he called.

'Gamefreaks? Isn't that what … we're meant to be?'

'Yow! We're gamers – a universe away. You can tell a gamefreak a mile off. They're only interested in Fasting up to the eyeballs while gaming. And any old game will do them.'

'I thought only spacers did Fast.'

Zeb threw one hand up, indicating the place in general. 'Tell *them* that.'

Willis bent down and began gathering up the fallen games.

'And don't bother picking them up. They've got staff for that.' Shaking his head, Zeb turned back to his stack of games. His personal Zeepad lay by his side and he picked it up and pushed it against one game after another, examining the details on the screen.

Willis left the fallen games neatly stacked on the floor and stood up in time to spot Arizona emerge from a nearby aisle and stroll towards them, her big eyes shining. She was elfin and fair-haired, and was dressed in stylish hyperboard gear – long white gloves and a matching sleeveless top and shorts.

'You both off sick too?' she said.

With no slots left in the rack, she gripped her hyperboard – the new kind, sheet-metal thin – under one arm. Her hyperboard gloves stretched almost to her bare shoulders. Willis had seen nothing like them before. She glanced at him and he felt his face burning. He couldn't think of anything to say.

Zeb kept his head down and studied his Zeepad screen. 'Hi, Ari,' he said, his voice cool. 'Stalking us?'

She laughed. 'Hardly.'

'Sure,' said Zeb. 'And that's why you followed us out the window. And that's why you've been searching for us up and down every aisle. Just so you can now waltz past accidentally on purpose.'

She gave an offhand shrug. 'Actually I'm doing you a favour. I thought you might like to know your departure didn't go unnoticed.'

Zeb waved carelessly. 'We already knew you knew.'

'I don't mean *me*. I mean Loveland. She was parking her car as you two kactoheads made your great escape. I watched her watching.'

Zeb's pause was brief. 'Nothing we can't handle.' He returned his attention to his Zeepad.

She pursed her lips. 'All right then.' She turned down a corner and disappeared.

'Did she just say Ms Loveland saw us?' Willis whispered. He felt sick at the thought.

'Big deal,' Zeb said without looking up.

Willis surveyed the end of the aisle, waiting for a reappearance of Arizona's slight form, but she didn't return. 'Do you and Arizona hang out?'

'No way.' Zeb didn't offer any explanation.

'Why not?' Willis prompted.

'Forget about her.' Zeb climbed to his feet, grasping a pile of games. 'I've got what we need.'

Willis dragged his gaze from the last point where Arizona had been visible and gaped at the clutch of first-person shooters in Zeb's hands. The top one had a moving image of a wolfman in leather straps and studs. It ripped into the neck of a human victim with its jagged teeth. Blood sprayed everywhere.

'What? All of them?' said Willis. 'And they look a bit … vicious. I'm not sure my mum—'

Zeb marched off. 'Let's see how many your Zeepad can handle.'

Willis followed more slowly. Up ahead he spied a life-size display of the strange man from the holo-ad he'd deleted.

Zeb nodded to it as he passed it. 'No need for that

place now,' he said, waving the clutch of games in the air. He looked pleased with himself.

Like the holo-ad, the placard display shifted in and out of focus, and gazing directly at it hurt Willis's eyes. One of its arms was fully extended and pointed to the store's exit. Under the figure were the words *Come to Virtualitee. Yip yip yippee.*

Behind the front counter stood a dishevelled man whose pallor suggested too many late-night gaming sessions. Zeb placed his stack of games on the counter and the man bent over them, checking the security seal on each. Then, without looking up, he held out a hand. 'Zeepad,' he grunted. He rubbed his unshaven chin.

When Willis didn't move, Zeb elbowed him.

'Oh, sorry.' Willis dug in his bag and produced his Zeepad. Zeb took it from him and handed it to the man for scanning. The man thrust it into a blue beam that rose from the counter's surface. The Zeepad squawked like an irate seagull.

Zeb turned to Willis. 'What's the matter with it?' he demanded.

Willis shrugged, perplexed. He'd never heard it make that sound before.

The man checked the Zeepad's screen, looked Willis and Zeb up and down, then pushed the stack of games to one side, away from them. 'You're underage,' he said.

Zeb seemed stunned. 'Can't you just ignore that?'

The man raised his eyebrows. 'Of course I can – but I won't.'

'Why not?' The agitation in Zeb's voice was obvious.

'Not at fifteen. If you were closer to eighteen, maybe. Those are all Xtreme-rated horrocore shooters you've got there. I can't sell stuff like that to minors.' He picked up the one with the wolfman. 'Look at this!' In the moving image, the creature now pulled an ugly weapon from a holster at its furry hip and fired. Then a shot came from somewhere else, something firing back. The wolfman's head erupted in an explosion of blood. The title ran across the top of the cover: *BANG!!! YOU'RE!!! DEAD!!!* The man threw the game down again. 'This Zeepad records everything about me, right down to what I had for breakfast and what I'd rather have had if I didn't have to rush off to work and deal with irritating kids like you two. If I let you guys buy these games and you get caught, you get slapped on the wrist. I get jail.'

Zeb ran his fingers through his hair. 'Can't I have *any?*' Willis could see the desperation in his eyes.

'Maybe we can get something else?' Willis said quietly. He was secretly relieved.

Zeb glared at Willis, then turned back to the man. 'There must be something I can do. Please. I'm begging you.'

The man's face softened. He stroked his stubbly chin again thoughtfully. 'I could call your parents. If they're happy to give me verbal approval ...'

Zeb's head dropped. 'My father's spacefronting.'

'Your mum?'

'No way! She's ... sick.' Zeb indicated Willis. 'But his dad used to be a bigwig in the security business. Buckets of money. He even bought him his own Plush.'

'That's very nice. But will he give permission to rent Xtreme horrocore?'

Zeb turned to Willis, a plea in his eyes.

'I don't think this is something my dad would be keen on,' Willis mumbled. 'We're not even meant to be here.'

Zeb dismissed him with an irritated wave and pointed back towards the display for the Virtualitee store. 'What about this other place?' he asked the man behind the counter. 'Hang on. Where'd it go?'

Willis tracked his gaze and saw what Zeb saw: nothing. The placard was gone.

'What other place?' asked the man. 'Why would we want to advertise some other place? Like we don't need the customers.' He sounded impatient. Without waiting for an answer, he walked off.

'Where's it gone?' Willis asked.

Zeb rounded on him. 'How should I know? We can't call my mother – she'll be senseless by this time of morning. But what's wrong with yours?'

'I didn't know your mum was sick.'

'Forget her, I'm asking about yours. You won't even try? Say you're on a school outing. Mothers believe anything.'

Willis thought about how pleased she'd be if she realised he was with a friend. But later, when she saw the games ... He shook his head slowly. 'As soon as she saw what I brought home, she'd be really unhappy.'

Zeb glowered. *'Really unhappy?* What the hell! If you were a real gamemate we'd be un-gamemating right about now.'

'But we can still play the Plush, right?'

'Yeah? With what? All you've got is rubbish.'

Willis grappled for an answer. 'If you don't want to game up, maybe we could just hang out?'

Zeb looked horrified. 'Hang out? Like where?'

Embarrassed, Willis looked at the floor. 'The Floating Baths are always good.'

'Floating around in the Bubble Arena, I suppose?'

'Actually, the Bubble Arena kind of freaks me out.'

Zeb shook his head. 'You amaze me,' he muttered.

Then he swivelled on his feet, retrieved his hyperboard from the rack and strode towards the exit. 'So long. Have a nice life.' He left the store without looking back.

Willis remained rooted to the spot for what seemed like an eternity, then suddenly realised this was the closest he'd ever got to having a friend. He grabbed his hyperboard from the rack and ran for the door. It opened in time for him to see a ziptram in the process of dumping to the ground, its doors shrieking open. And there was Zeb, marching towards it.

'Wait!' Willis yelled at both the ziptram and Zeb. Knowing ziptrams wait for no one, he shoved his bag into position behind him, slammed his hyperboard to the ground, and jumped on. Kicking it back, he raced towards the ziptram's entrance. Zeb climbed its steps. Willis leant forward heavily for maximum speed. If he'd had time to think about it, he'd never have attempted the manoeuvre he was now planning.

The ziptram's door began to close, the shrieking sound mixing with the piercing screech of the vehicle as it lurched from the ground. Willis tilted and smashed through the remaining crack, little more than a slice of air, and landed on the bottom step. He grabbed his hyperboard and scrambled up the steps.

From where the trampilot sat in his tiny cockpit, he gawped at Willis, clearly astounded. 'Get strapped in, ya clown,' he growled. The door sealed shut and the tram accelerated with a roar.

The other passengers were already locked into safety seats or strapped into harnesses against the walls. Willis clung to one passenger after another as he worked his way down the aisle, ignoring their astonished faces. He spied Zeb in the very back seat, an automatic safety bar descending over him. Zeb waved when he saw Willis, and shoved his hands under the lowering bar, trying to prevent it from descending further. He could see Zeb straining, slowly losing the battle. Willis gave up clinging to passengers and darted towards Zeb, pushing back his fear – he'd never been out of a harness or safety seat on a moving ziptram before. It wasn't just the penalties that worried him – he'd heard the stories: broken necks, cracked skulls ... What was it about Zeb? His mother would be horrified if she knew the things Willis had done since meeting him.

The safety bar whined as Zeb pushed back at it, his face taut with effort. With only a few more steps to go, Willis leapt and landed next to Zeb and beneath the bar. Zeb released it. It slammed down over them, locking into place.

Willis dropped his hyperboard at his feet, next to Zeb's. 'You can borrow my Plush,' he gasped. 'We can game up at your place.'

Zeb stared in surprise. 'Your mum would allow that?'

'I won't tell her.'

Zeb nodded his approval. 'I guess you can still tag along then.' He looked Willis in the eye and snickered. 'Under one condition.'

'What?'

'Never suggest the Floating Baths to me again. Gaming up is what I'm into. Gaming up's my life. Floating Baths! And you don't even do the Bubble Arena.'

They both laughed and Willis felt a wave of relief wash over him. They were still friends.

'There's still the problem of where to get games from,' Zeb mused.

At that moment a deep, lurching sound, like a small earth tremor, came from behind them. Then a low voice spoke: 'Floating Baths? Indeed.'

Willis and Zeb looked at each other.

'I thought we were in the back seat?' Willis whispered.

'We are,' said Zeb.

Chapter 4

Before Willis could stop him, Zeb twisted awkwardly in his seat, making the safety bar whine. 'What on earth?' he said. 'You!'

Willis followed Zeb's startled gaze and stared directly into the impenetrable sunglasses and face of the man from the Plush holo-ad. The man from Virtualitee, grey, bald and shrouded in a long, black overcoat. The safety bar had not come down around him, yet he sat relaxed and casual, unaffected by the sudden drops and sideways lurches of the speeding tram.

And there was something else. Something that Willis had considered a fault in the holo-ad and the display that had mysteriously vanished, yet now witnessed again. Like the holo-ad, like the display, the man shifted in and out of focus.

The man turned to Willis and spoke. 'There's no

need for feckless frolicking at the Floating Baths.'

'Pardon?'

He grinned. 'Come to Virtualitee. Come and get your freebie jeebies.'

Willis swallowed, a muddle of confusion and fear rising in him. 'How did you get there? I thought *we* were in the back seat.'

The man leant forward. 'If you're in the back seat, then where am I? In the boot?'

Willis wondered how the man could see anything through the solid black lenses of his glasses.

'Do you want your freebie or not?' the man asked.

'No!' said Willis at the same time as Zeb said, 'Yes!'

Zeb turned to Willis. 'We can at least hear him out.'

The man smiled at Zeb and extended his arm, two skeletal fingers and a thumb pinched together as if he held something. 'My card,' he said. But Willis could see only air.

Zeb slowly brought his hand up.

'Zeb? What are you doing?' Willis asked.

Zeb paused and looked at him. 'It's just a card.'

Willis stiffened. 'I can't see one.'

Zeb knitted his eyebrows and stared at the man's fingers. 'I can. Sort of.'

'You can?' The man sounded pleased. 'Good.' But

43

when Zeb didn't move, he added: 'Are you going to take it or not?'

Zeb reached forward, a look of concentration on his face. Instead of grasping at the air before the man's fingers, where Willis could see no card, Zeb touched his fingertips. The man jerked away, clutching his hand and hissing and spitting. Zeb too pulled away with a jolt. He rubbed his own hand. 'I couldn't see the card well enough.'

'So you thought you'd assault me? Your hands. They were warm and ... clammy.' He spoke his last words in disgust.

Willis watched the man rock from side to side, bent over and nursing his hand. Under his clutching fingers, his skin appeared to be moving, bubbling and shifting. He looked up at Zeb and a smile formed on his pallid face. 'Still,' he said, 'no pain, no game.'

'Gain,' Willis corrected.

'Gain or game,' the man said and shrugged his wide shoulders. 'All the same to me.'

Zeb didn't pay them any attention. He held something small and square. The card. Willis could see it now. Zeb was examining it closely.

'What does this entitle us to?' asked Zeb. He looked at the man. 'I'm only interested in first-person shooters. Horrocore ones.'

'Horrocore!' The man let go of his injured hand and Willis noticed his grey skin was smooth once more. 'What a coincidence, that's my speciality. Well, it is now, anyway.'

Willis pressed closer to Zeb for a better view of the card. It was zipanimated, changing colour constantly. Unlike the man, it did not shift in and out of focus. The words *Come to Virtualitee and see for yourself* wriggled across its surface.

When he looked around again, the man was cradling an electric guitar.

'Where'd you get that from?' Willis said, astonished.

The ziptram jerked, throwing Willis and Zeb against their safety bar. The man was unaffected. He grasped one end of a cord attached to the guitar. 'Let me see,' he said, 'where can I plug this in? Ah, yes, indeedy.'

He plugged it into the empty air, where it remained suspended by nothing, and began to strum, the strings fizzing and crackling like a wet firecracker. He leant towards Zeb and Willis, half singing, half growling. 'Come to Virtualitee and see for yourself.' Then he threw his head back and sang at full throttle. 'Ooh, I went to Virtualitee and I saw for myself.' Willis and Zeb winced, but the man stopped suddenly. He faced the tram window and the rushing city view. 'Ah! Is that a storm I hear? Lovely. A veritable torrent.'

'No,' said Willis, glancing out. 'It's not raining at all.'

Zeb peered at the card in his hand again. '*Horrocore* is even written here. And it says it's all free. That can't be right.'

The man pushed his face next to Zeb's. 'But it is! Well, *virtually*, anyway. We trade at another level. Come to Virtualitee and see. It's a mere hyperboard-dash away. Come any night. But it must be night, mind. I'll be there to greet you myself.' Then he turned to Willis. 'You are quite correct. In Virtualitee, it never rains. But it roars. Wailing, howling … ululating even. Gamers all over the world – a tempest of gamefreaks, speaking collectively – engaging with the elements. Burning. Drowning. Suffocating. Sinking.'

Willis stared at him open-mouthed. The man was bewildering. 'Gamefreaks and gamers aren't the same thing,' he said finally.

'Don't get picky picky,' the man replied. He stood, swinging his guitar to his back with a shrug. At the same moment, red letters fixed to the tram wall flashed an urgent message: *Dumpdown alert! Dumpdown alert!*

'You'd better strap in,' Willis said. Standing in the aisle during a dumpdown was perilous.

Zeb tucked his card between his legs and they braced themselves against the safety bar as the ziptram jerked in a sudden forward motion, wrenched upward, and finally thrust downwards, shuddering. Through the whole dumpdown process, the man remained standing, impervious to the thrusts and the final plunge. Willis had not thought such a thing was possible. The man moved down the aisle until he stood alongside Willis. He raised one hand to him, his fingers poised as if he held something. Again, Willis could see nothing.

'Take it,' Zeb said over his shoulder.

'Take what?'

'It's a game! Zoomin.'

'I can't see anything.'

'Let me.' Zeb pushed Willis down, almost crushing him in his eagerness to take what the man was offering.

The man hissed and pulled back slightly. 'Careful.'

This time Zeb didn't touch the man's hand. Instead, he grasped the air in front of the skeletal fingers. Then he dropped back into his seat.

Willis straightened and watched the man continue down the aisle. He moved with a fluid, gliding motion that took him through the shrieking door. He didn't look back.

'Well what did you think of that?' he asked Zeb.

'What?' Zeb was concentrating on a game he now held.

Willis frowned, scratching his head. 'Could you see him holding that?'

'Of course.'

Willis couldn't fully make out the cover. Animals of some kind flew across a sky in attack formation. One word, the title no doubt, ran across the top: *EleMental*.

'Is it really a game? Just like that, he gave us one?'

'It's a demo, I guess.'

Willis sighed. 'How's your hand?'

'Fine.'

'Then why are you rubbing it?'

Zeb stopped his rubbing and shuffled away from Willis.

'The guy was a total neghead, don't you think?' Willis persisted.

But Zeb didn't answer. He placed the game between his knees and looked at the card once more. 'So this is Virtualitee.' He spoke quietly, as if to himself. 'And it specialises in horrocore.' He ran his fingertips over the card's surface, caressing it.

'Show us.'

Zeb ignored him.

Willis leant over for a better look. Different words continued to wriggle across the card's surface. He saw the word *Virtualitee* again. Two other words caught his attention: *Grimble Dower.* The man's name? It must be. Two words slid under his name: *Virtual Greetings.* Then *Juicy Carnage* jigged about under that. And: *Blood! Gore!* Images wound around the animated words: slender eels with pinprick eyes; gyrating skeletons brandishing cutlasses; zombie dogs with teeth like steak knives ... Pictures of what was on offer, Willis guessed.

'Turn it over,' Willis said.

Zeb flipped the card, still holding it close. On the back were directions showing how to get there. It was an active map; it gave directions from where they were now. The directions changed smoothly, keeping pace with the ziptram's journey. A moving dot blinked on a street on the outskirts of the map.

Zeb pointed at it. 'That has to be us.'

Willis nodded and pointed to a stationary dot on the opposite side. 'It's bit more than a hyperboard-dash away.'

It was also a singing card, and, complete with squeaky trumpets, it chose to sing out just then: '*Come to Virtualitee and see for yourself. Ooh indeedy. Yip, yip!*' The voice was a high, squeaky version of Grimble Dower's. '*I went to Virtualitee and I saw for myself. Yippy, yippy, yip, yip.*' The card fell silent.

Zeb tucked it away, picked up the game and shook it. 'This should keep us going for the time being. Wanna stay overnight at my place?'

Willis couldn't hold back his smile. 'Your place? Sure! On the weekend?'

'Tonight, kactohead. And we can game through the night. My mother couldn't give a rats what I did.'

Willis laughed. 'Okay. I'll check with my mum as soon as I get home from school.'

'School? We're not going back there. How long will it take us to pick up your stuff from your place? An hour? Or maybe half an hour, if we really hurry?'

'Don't you think we should put in a bit of an appearance back at school?'

Zeb sighed. 'You can if you want.'

'I'll come as soon as I can. After school.'

'Whatever. Just don't forget the Plush.'

The Plush. Of course. That was all Zeb was really after. Willis's smile faded. But he nodded anyway.

CHAPTER 5

Willis had the perfect distraction from potentially inquisitive eyes as he ran through the school grounds. Deep clouds that had been grumbling overhead for some time finally broke in a stinging deluge. He hurried through it, scrambled through the same small window he'd crawled out of earlier, and dropped onto the floor of the female toilets. But he was soaked through – evidence that he'd been outside when no one in their right mind would have been. His sodden state would invite awkward questions.

He dried off as best as he could in a toilet cubicle and then slipped into the corridor. Where to now? He hastened down one corridor after another until he reached a room reserved during lunch hours for the Griffin Attax Club. It was always warm and musty in there. It would give his clothes time to dry some more.

The hubbub of chatter greeted him as he entered, pushing his sopping hair back from his face and acting as nonchalant as possible.

Students sat around illuminated game boards, chatting, laughing and playing Griffin Attax. The game pieces – griffins, dragons, unicorns, yetis, trolls – dodged, twisted and fought across boards displaying a variety of medieval landscapes featuring mountainous terrains, ancient forests, soft green hills, all dotted with crumbling, grey battlements. The formations of the pieces varied from one-on-one bouts to all-out mob brawls, depending on the commands – issued covertly by hand signals, whispers or under the table controls – from the players.

Willis was lucky enough to find a spot towards the back. He made for it and switched the board on. It lit up – a rural village scene, with the obligatory timeworn battlement – and the pieces materialised in a scattered mess across it. Willis gathered them up. They wriggled in his fingers. He stared at the board, uncertain where to place them. He could feel the rainwater trickle through his matted hair and dribble from the tip of his nose. The pieces let out tiny hollers and writhed in his careful grip as they attempted to avoid the colossal, splattering globs. With no idea what to do next, Willis returned the creatures to the board and hoped they'd sort things out for themselves.

Then a voice above him said: 'You going to play or are you just going to sit there and drizzle all over a perfectly good game?'

Willis looked up into the sneering face of a kid he didn't know. He looked older than Willis by a few years – seventeen at least. Another boy stood behind him, about the same age.

'I was here first,' Willis mumbled. But inside he was preparing to leave. He hated fights. The best way out, he knew, was to lose them as quickly as you could and get the hell out of there.

'And now we're here,' the second boy said. 'The point is, there are two of us and there's only one of you. So why don't you leave the gaming to people who know how to?'

They moved closer and were about to gather up the pieces when someone spoke from behind them. Female. Confident. 'Sorry I'm late!' she said. 'Good, you've started warming up the pieces.'

The two boys parted to reveal Arizona. She still wore her white hyperboard gear – the long gloves and matching top, a belt for her Zeepad and tight, white shorts that ended just below the knee – but she no longer clutched her thin hyperboard.

She nodded to them in a casual way. 'Kurt. Jake.' They nodded back as she manoeuvred around them and plonked herself into the chair opposite Willis.

'Sorry, Ari,' Kurt – the first boy – said. 'We didn't know this was your place.'

'That's fine,' Arizona said. 'No harm done.' She turned away, obviously dismissing them. But they remained where they were.

'This has to be the first time we've seen you in here,' Kurt said.

'First time for everything, boys.' She didn't look at them as she spoke. 'Oh, and by the way,' she added, 'my name's *Arizona* not *Ari*.' When they still didn't move she turned to them. 'You can go now,' she said with a gracious smile.

'Oh. Yes. Sorry.' They moved off.

Willis watched them weave around the other tables and, with no game board table available, eventually leave the room. When he looked back, he saw that Arizona was watching him from across the table of aimlessly wandering game pieces.

'Thank you,' he said.

'You're welcome. You looked as if you could do with some help.'

It was a ridiculous gesture and he didn't know what made him do it. But he leant forward and extended a hand. 'I'm Willis,' he said. As soon as he did it he wanted to kick himself. And her reaction was the worst thing imaginable. She jerked her hand away and pulled back as if repulsed.

'Sorry.' His face burnt with embarrassment.

'I already know who you are,' she said. 'We're in the same class for some things, remember?' She placed a hand palm-up on the table. A tiny black goblin with a sword and a small hairy troll with a chain that ended in a miniature ball of spikes climbed onto her hand. She stroked them with a finger. They purred in response.

'It's just that, well, we've never spoken before today,' Willis explained. It surprised him she knew his name. Same classes or not. And it pleased him. Behind her, across the room, the long windows had steamed up. He could hear the rain pelting against the glass panes. 'You came back too?' he ventured. 'After Screamers.'

She shrugged. 'I come and go as I please.' She glanced over her shoulder at the closed door at the front of the room. 'So, who are you really waiting for?' she asked. 'Who's your no-show? Not Zeb, surely?'

With that last question, Willis came crashing back to earth. Of course, that was why she'd come over and sat down; she wanted to talk about Zeb.

She flicked her head in a gesture that took in the room. 'I'd never have thought to catch him in a place like this.'

Willis looked around, taking in the shapeless haircuts and clothes, the overall seriousness that hung over the place, and knew what she meant. Nice enough people but not the kind Zeb would want to hang out with. Willis had only known Zeb a short while, but he could tell that much already.

She pulled a face. 'Even the name of this game. Ugh.'

Willis didn't understand. 'What's wrong with it?'

'*Attacks* deliberately misspelt with an X? That's so L.A.M.E.'

'Yeah? And here was I thinking it was K.U.L.E.'

She made as if to vomit. Two fingers in her open mouth.

Willis made a wry face. 'To tell you the truth I wasn't waiting for anyone. I'm trying to get dry. I didn't expect it to be this crowded. It's because of the rain, I guess.'

He wiped at his hair with his wet sleeve, a useless act. 'You were outside like me and Zeb,' he said. 'But you're not even wet.'

She tapped the Zeepad attached to her waist. 'I check the forecasts.'

'Oh.'

They looked at each other for a moment in silence.

A purple dragon spiralled up from the board. It corkscrewed in the air before their faces and then in one big loop ducked under the table. Willis crouched down to fetch it, grateful for the distraction. He took care not to knock the row of coloured player buttons fixed under the table and found himself staring directly at Arizona's feet. Her hyperboard runners, one settled on top of the other, were petite. The dragon peeped out from behind them.

'I saw you at the Floating Baths the other day,' she said. Though he remained hunched under the table, her voice was surprisingly near. He banged his head on the table's underside as he looked up and into her blue-green eyes. She was bending down, her palm outstretched. The dragon piece ran over and hopped onto it.

They sat back up in their chairs.

'And I know you saw me,' she continued, 'but you kept looking away when I tried to catch your eye.'

Willis did remember that. 'I didn't think you were looking at me.' Never in a quadrillion years had he thought that.

'Well, I was. You were someone I knew from school and I was trying to say "hi".' The dragon piece unfurled its wings, shook them, and sashayed from her hand and onto the board. 'Go on now,' she said to it, prodding it gently. 'Join the others. Look, what about them?' She gestured to a group of unicorns and Pan gods who were looking lost without a player to direct them. The dragon bleated and ran over to join them.

'I didn't see Zeb with you though,' she added. 'Was he there? I didn't think it was his thing.'

Ah, Willis thought. Zeb again. 'I didn't know Zeb then. We've really only hung out a couple of times. We're not that close.' Willis eyed her. 'How long have *you* known him?' She wanted to talk about Zeb; that was clear. He might as well accommodate her.

'A long time,' she said. Her gaze grew distant. 'Since we were toddlers, in fact. And we were friends too. Once.'

'And now?'

She gestured with her empty hands. 'And now we're not. End of story. Do you mind if we don't talk about Zeb anymore? I'm sick of hearing about him.'

'Really?'

'Who wouldn't be? Straight-A student more years running than any other kid in the universe—'

'I didn't know that.'

'—hyperboard champion—'

'*And* a hyperboard champion?'

'Well, nearly was.' She sighed. 'But like I said, let's drop the subject.'

You're the one that asked about him, Willis wanted to say. Or maybe he was being unfair? Perhaps it was just because Zeb was something they had in common. He snuck a glance at her. Something about her manner reminded him of Zeb. Both of them seemed quick to know what's what. And had no trouble telling him.

With a gesture of his hand, he indicated her hyperboard gear. 'You're obviously a good hyperboarder yourself.'

She looked uncomfortable at that. 'I'm not, I'm rubbish. This is just for looks.'

The purple light announcing that classes were about to start flashed from a corner of the room.

She stood up. 'We'd better go.'

Willis worried he might have offended her somehow. No one usually responded so quickly when it was time to get back to class. She waved goodbye to the game pieces and they waved back as she switched the board off. They dematerialised, still waving.

Other students packed up and slowly climbed to their feet as Willis and Arizona worked their way around the tables and entered the corridor. It was filling with students.

'Willis,' she said, suddenly turning to him and looking at him seriously. 'I didn't just find you in there by accident, you know.'

'Oh?' Here it comes, he thought. Whatever it was she really wanted from him.

'I saw you head in and followed you. I've enjoyed chatting to you. It's great to have someone new around here. I've known everyone else since kindergarten. Plus, I've seen you wagging already! Talk to me next time you see me, okay? At the Baths or wherever.'

Willis swallowed. Was she thanking him for talking to her? 'Er, sure, Arizona.'

She smiled. 'And you can call me Ari. My friends do.' She said these last words as she moved off, giving Willis no chance to respond. He didn't know how to anyway.

He watched her disappear and reappear as fellow students milled around. After a while, the growing bustle swallowed her up.

Willis opened his mouth. 'Okay … Ari,' he said to nobody. When he turned and strode in the other direction, towards his class, he was dancing on the moon.

CHAPTER 6

Willis arrived at Zeb's door later that evening, carrying his dad's overnight bag. He held his Plush under one arm, wrapped in an old sheet.

Zeb let him into a pokey entrance hall with a glass sliding door to one side and a dim corridor on his right. A lean, spent-looking woman stood there – his mother, Willis assumed. Something about her pose told him she'd not been waiting to greet him. More likely, she'd been caught hurrying past. Willis took in her frayed, pink dressing-gown. She held a glass tumbler at an angle and red wine dripped from it. He could see new red stains rolling down the front of her dressing-gown. His gaze kept sliding to them.

'This is Mum,' Zeb said.

'I'm off to bed,' she said in a dry voice. Her frown accentuated her gauntness. 'Help yourselves to anything from the fridge.' She indicated an open door behind her, adjacent to the sliding door. Beyond it, Willis could see part of a dining area.

They both nodded.

She moved off and disappeared through a door halfway down the corridor.

'She gets tired easily,' Zeb said quietly, though Willis had said nothing.

There was a scuffling sound and Zeb glanced towards the open dining-room door. 'And that's Spud. My seven-year-old brother. He likes to stick in the background.'

Willis couldn't see anyone.

'Come on out, Spud,' Zeb said. 'I know you're there.'

A stocky boy with a chop-top haircut emerged from the shadow of the small gap between the dining-room door and the wall. He stood for a brief moment looking at Willis, made as if to nod, but then instead ran down the corridor and through a bedroom door just before a bend.

Zeb's expression remained blank. 'Well, that was Spud,' he said.

Willis gazed after the boy, wondering how it must feel to have a brother, one more person in your family. So it wasn't just you.

At Zeb's suggestion, they skipped dinner and headed straight for his bedroom. Willis pushed his hunger pangs to the back of his mind. Zeb's room was small, with a graffiti-etched wooden bed head, tangled bed sheets, a box with wires and different-sized tools spilling from it, open dresser drawers with clothes hanging out … His gaze rested on a peeling zeeposter on the wall by the bed, displaying a frenzied musician swinging his guitar like a heavy axe. The guitar shattered in a spray of sparks each time it hit the stage's wooden boards. After each shattering, the poster's image flicked back and the guitarist swung again. *Kerrr-rackk* … flick … *Kerrr-rackk*.

Beneath the poster – in fact directly beneath the spraying sparks – sat an old console on a plastic crate.

Willis laughed. 'This your DVP? It's as if the guy in the poster's smashing it.'

Zeb didn't say anything.

Willis moved closer for a better look at the console. There was a large gash in its front; tape partially masked it. The name of the console was fixed to the opposite corner: *Magnum 50*. 'I didn't think they made Magnums anymore.' Too late, Willis bit his tongue. He looked around in time to see Zeb glancing away, gazing out the window.

'They don't,' Zeb said.

'Well,' Willis said after a moment, 'we've got my Plush now. Where shall I put it?'

'Hold on.' Zeb pushed in front of Willis and grabbed the old console. Bending down, he tried shoving it under his bed with his foot, but it refused to go. Willis could see a lot of clutter under there already. A well-aimed kick from Zeb eventually got it under. Then he pointed to the space left on the crate. 'There looks like a good spot.'

Willis pulled the sheet from his Plush and carefully set it down. He'd barely stood back when Zeb stepped in front of him and knelt before the white machine, one hand hovering over it. He paused as if savouring the moment. Then he rubbed one side in a circular motion. The console's tiny lights blinked a few times and a cluster of multicoloured beams rose up, laser meters with titles hovering over them: *Speed, Tactics, Difficulty, eLusions, Weapons, Sonic capacity, Real-time physics.*

'Set: max,' Zeb said. The tips of the meters darkened. 'And while we're about it.' He rubbed the console's surface again. More beams rose from the console. They reminded Willis of a nighttime cityscape. Titles materialised over them: *Brutality, Ferocity, Malice, Hostility, Violence, Aggression, Gore, Endurance, Suffering, Deception, Antagonism, Deceit, Desperation, Torment, Agony* ... Too many for Willis to read.

'Set all: max,' Zeb said. 'And save settings.'

The tips of the bristling meters darkened and the meters withdrew.

Zeb sat back with a satisfied expression. 'Right,' he said, 'let's game up.'

CHAPTER 7

After a crash of music, a single, bold word materialised over their heads.

EleMental

The letters shattered into pieces and, from somewhere off-gamespace, an oil-black dragon swept into the room, its forelegs and talons extended. This close, its giant, beating wings, rooted to its muscular, scaly back, were largely out of view. Their beating was a continuous *whomph* that hammered in their ears. On its rolling head sat a golden crown; it glinted behind its stubby horns and above its searching, emerald eyes. Willis saw its gaze register them and two jets of flame flared from its nostrils as fiery whipsnakes that tried to strike at them.

Willis dropped to his knees, crouching and peering up through his fingers. Zeb barely moved. He evaded the striking flames with ease, smiling broadly, and shifting his head and shoulders only as necessary.

When the dragon swept back off-gamespace, Willis heard his own piercing shriek; he heard it in a removed way, as if he'd fled his body.

Zeb grinned down at him, his hands on his hips. 'Screaming can be fun. But this is just the credits.'

Willis became aware of music, it picked up a beat, growing into an electro-thrash thumping. And new words floated into the room.

First EleMental: The Hall of the Mountain Dragon

Then smaller words: *Produced by Grimble Dower. Directed by Grimble Dower. From an idea by Gr—*

'Attention game,' Zeb snapped. 'Skip credits.'

The words disappeared and the music dropped to nothing. After a pause a voice spoke. Male. Polite. Vaguely familiar. 'Number of gamers?'

'Two,' said Zeb.

'Opponents in combat with one another?'

Zeb looked Willis up and down. 'Better not,' he said. 'Make it co-op.'

'Names?'

'Zeb,' said Zeb and looked expectantly at Willis.

'Oh, erh, and Willis,' said Willis.

Zeb smiled softly. 'Attention, game. Correction. Cut: *Oh erh and Willis*. Replace: *Willis*.'

Willis nodded a *thank you*, too fearful to speak.

The four walls and ceiling of Zeb's bedroom melted away. They stood in a hot, scrubby wasteland. Willis squinted in the brightness.

Zeb spread his arms wide. 'Whoa! Check out these eLusions. This is zipgen physics at its best. The frame rate must be insane! And this heat is … hot.'

'Score,' said the game voice. 'Zeb: zero; Willis: zero; mountain dragon: zero.'

'What's this over here?' Zeb said. He ran over to something on the ground and took a deep whiff. 'Phwoar! That's gotta be the worst, best, highest-res rotting dead animal I've ever laid eyes on. Fan-zoomin-tastic.'

Willis sidled over, looked and looked away. Black bugs, some shiny and hard, others long and soft, swarmed over a rank carcass, feasting on its internal organs. It was hard to identify what the creature might once have been. A hound of some kind?

Zeb had already moved on, looking bored. He threw his head up to the sky. Then he gazed down at the parched ground, his brow knitted. He kicked at some stones. He stuffed his hands in his pockets and puffed out his cheeks. Finally, he looked at Willis, who had been watching him. 'Hell,' he said. 'I hate slow beginnings. Where's the horrocore? Any monsters will do.' He looked around again. This time something in the distance caught his attention. He stared at the horizon and pointed. 'The draw distance is immense. What's that way, way over there?'

Willis squinted into the far-off scrub but couldn't see anything.

'It's got to be where this level's boss enemy is,' Zeb said. 'Come on.' He set off at a run without looking back.

Willis followed at a slower pace, doing his best to make out what Zeb had pointed at. In the distance, the vague outline of a cliff emerged, a mere shade in difference from its scrubby surroundings. Zeb now stood at its base, a small figure gazing up at the vastness.

'It's okay to talk now,' Zeb said, when Willis finally reached him. 'The game's not in attention mode.'

'Thanks.' Willis stared at the cliff towering over him. He knew his Plush was good and now he was finding out just how good.

'This is all a bit more platformery than I usually like.'

Willis didn't understand. 'What do you mean?'

'The game.' He pointed up. 'See that cave mouth up there? That's our next objective: get to the platform in front of it.'

It took a while, but eventually Willis spied an opening behind a rock ledge two thirds of the way up. He swallowed. 'Zeb, don't tell me we have to—' He fell silent, reluctant to finish his words.

'On my old DVP, this cliff face wouldn't be a quarter of this size. You could jump over it.' He patted Willis on the shoulder. 'Don't worry, Wil Boy, once we're through that hole, I'm sure there'll be plenty of shooter action. That quick sprint across the desert? A warm-up test. Let's see if I've unlocked something.'

'Please don't call me *Wil Boy*,' Willis mumbled.

Zeb laughed and set about hunting around. Sure enough, he found and quickly dragged out climbing harnesses and other pieces of equipment from behind a row of scraggy bushes. In keeping with the Plush, the equipment looked advanced: autoropes and wizzpicks.

Zeb threw on the gear and sent the wizzpick off on its own up the cliff face with one end of the rope attached to it – *chink, chink, chink, chink, chink*. He snatched up the other end and held it against his waist. The rope snaked itself securely about the buckles of his harness. The wizzpick continued chattering up the incline like a crazed woodpecker and stopped when the rope was taut. Zeb waved goodbye and yanked at the rope.

'See ya later, Wil Boy.' He bounded up the cliff.

Willis turned to his own gear and found his autorope had secured itself about a rock the size of a football. It took some effort to prise the rope free. When he finally managed it, he held the rope to his waist and watched with relief as it snaked through the buckles of his harness. But at the last moment, it wrapped itself about the rock again. This time, no matter how hard Willis tried, he couldn't free it. Giving in, he left it dangling heavily from his side and double-checked his wizzpick was attached to the other end of the rope. He noticed a sliding switch set into one side of the pick's wooden handle. Settings! He set it to *slow* and sent the small tool up the cliff face – *chink ... chink ... chink ... chink ... chink* – and began the ascent. The rock banged against his hip.

'Score,' said the game voice. 'Zeb: five; Willis: zero; mountain dragon: zero.'

Zeb must have defeated a minor beast, Willis realised. He checked his rigging, adjusted his straps, did his best to push the swinging rock into a more comfortable position, and continued his climb.

The voice came again: 'Score – Zeb: fifteen; Willis: zero; mountain dragon: zero.'

Ten more points. More than a minor beast, that one, then. Willis kept climbing.

'Score – Zeb: twenty-five; Willis: zero; mountain dragon: zero.'

Another ten! Zeb was roaring through this game. At least the dragon was doing as badly as Willis was.

'Score—'

Willis groaned.

'Zeb: thirty-five—' The voice paused. 'Correction. Zeb: forty—' Another brief pause. 'Correction. Zeb: fifty-five; Willis: zero; mountain dragon: zero.'

'Hey!' Willis cried out. He almost lost his footing. Pieces of rock crumbled under his scrabbling feet and he watched them fall. 'Shut up with those scores.'

'Score—'

'Attention game,' he growled. 'Cut: score.'

'Ze—' The voice fell silent. But then it was back: 'No score count is inadvisable,' it said coolly. 'Reason: a gamer must know if he or she is winning.'

Willis stared into the craggy rock in front of his nose. *Winning?* he thought. *Not much chance of that.* 'Cut: score,' he repeated.

'Request denied,' the voice said. 'The point is to win. The score must be announced.'

'Oh yeah? I'll show you who's boss.' Willis almost slipped, but regained his footing. He took a breath.

'Plush? Are you there, Plush? Attention, Plush.'

'Plush here,' said a different voice. Female. It carried an air of authority.

'This is Willis, the Plush owner. Er, your owner.'

'Hello, Willis.'

'Override game instructions. No audio score.'

'Keeping score is a lower command belonging to a game.'

'Please. I'd really appreciate it.'

There was a pause.

'You are very polite. Request granted.'

Willis grinned. 'Thank you.'

He shifted the rock at his side and renewed his climb with more vigour. Though he hadn't defeated anything, he felt victorious. Minutes later, he pulled himself over the edge and lay slumped on the rock platform before the cave mouth. When he sat up, he untied the rope and let the rock tumble from him. The silent darkness of the cave waited a few metres away. He stood, rubbing the sore spot on his thigh, and edged towards it.

At the same moment, a scream pierced the silence. Long and travelling from deep within the gut of the cave, its journey through unseen tunnels stamping in it a rich echo. Willis leapt to one side of the cave entrance and crouched, but something about the scream told him it wasn't one of pain or fear. He imagined Zeb engaged in the final strokes of a frenetic battle. Zeb having a good time. Zeb in ecstasy.

Willis waited a few more moments, trying to relax, then cautiously entered the cave. He immediately stiffened. Something moved in the shadows ahead, deeper in the cave. A grey shape, barely discernible, distant but moving towards him. There! He could make out the evil yellow glint of its eyes. His fingers instinctively ran to his side and he discovered a holster at his right hip. He glanced down, surprised. A long, blood-red gun poked from the holster. Zeb was right, these eLusions were really something. Perhaps he should get the score tally going again after all?

The shape drew closer and Willis braced himself for battle. He grappled with the holster but couldn't release the clasp. Hell! He tried with both hands, catching a finger from his left hand in the gun's trigger. The creature continued towards him. Willis yanked at the gun with both hands, savagely pulling at it.

Zeb emerged from the darkness and stared at him in amusement. 'What are you up to?'

Willis jumped in fright – 'What?' – and twisted away. No way did he want Zeb to see his left hand caught in the gun. Glancing back over his shoulder, he gave an awkward wave with his right hand. 'Oh. Hi! Hang on a minute. I'm just—'

Zeb's hand came around and rested on Willis's left hand. 'Let me help you with that,' he said. With one smooth motion he freed Willis's hand.

Willis sighed with relief. And only then did he see Zeb's gleeful, maniacal expression, his wide eyes. The dragon's golden crown perched crookedly on his head. Two prongs fixed to either side of the crown glinted yellow in the light from the cave mouth. In his other hand, he gripped the dripping head of the black mountain dragon. Now and then, a feeble spark sputtered from a nostril.

'Game over?' Willis asked when he found his voice.

'Level. Or *EleMental*, as this game's calling them.' He pointed to the head. 'This handsome fella was guarding a secret door back there. That'll lead to the next EleMental. You ready?'

'Not just yet.'

Zeb turned and faced the cave opening and the burnt-orange vista of the wasteland beyond it. In one quick movement he punted the head through the cave's mouth. Willis watched it curve through the air and drop out of sight. Across the expanse, the sun tipped the fringes of the horizon. Its gleam outlined Zeb in a silhouette. From where Willis stood, Zeb, wearing the dragon's crown and etched in fire, seemed like a god.

Across the sky, across everything, a chime rang out.

Zeb turned to Willis. 'That'll be the door,' he said.

Chapter 8

Ding-dong. The chime sounded again.

Zeb burst from his bedroom and into the corridor.

Willis hurried after him. 'Do you usually get visitors at this hour?' he asked. He didn't know the exact time but he knew gaming chewed up the hours, making them shoot past like minutes. It could well be coming around to midnight.

'We don't get visitors any time,' Zeb replied, stretching his stride as if about to take on another game challenge. He reached the front door and yanked it open.

Willis stopped behind him.

A man stood on the step with his back to them. His breath steamed in the sour autumn air as he muttered something incoherent. A heavy orange and black object shaped like a small cannon hung diagonally across his back. It was smothered in red and white *Caution!* and *Danger!* symbols.

The man slowly turned and gazed blearily at Zeb. He possessed the sallow face and stoop common to all spacers, and wore the convict-like, moon-grey coveralls typical of an asteroid miner, complete with the insignia on the breast pocket of a sparking rock drill biting into a spinning asteroid. In the half-light, Willis could see tiny golden leaves stuck to the hard toes of his damp and blocky antigrav boots. He rolled his head, scratching at his oily blond hair. He seemed to be struggling to think, remembering how to form words. Then he spoke: 'Ah, I know who you are.' He kept his gaze fixed on Zeb, paying no attention to Willis. 'Your mum in?'

Zeb shrugged.

'Ya gotta tongue?'

Zeb gave another shrug. 'Maybe she is, maybe she isn't.'

Willis listened, shocked at Zeb's feigned non-chalance. Was he taking this guy on? This was no boss enemy you could repeatedly challenge until you defeated it. Or shut down and walk away from. This was real.

The man glowered, balling his fists, but seemed uncertain what to say.

Then Ms Redman's shaky voice travelled down the corridor as she approached from somewhere behind. 'Is everything all right?'

Willis turned and took her in as she stepped up. Her dressing-gown was mis-buttoned and her eyes widened in alarm.

'Lance?' she said. 'Oh God.'

The man grunted. 'Hello, Marce. I'm back earth-side.'

'What do you want?' she asked. And then without waiting for an answer, added, 'Zeb, you and your friend go back to your room. Now, please.' She spoke without looking at them, manoeuvring in front of them.

Zeb straightened, affronted. 'Not until you explain who this man is.'

The man – Lance – curled his upper lip and seemed about to step forwards, towards Zeb. But Zeb's mother got in first. 'Leave this to me,' she said in a fierce whisper.

Zeb slowly shook his head, his face set. 'Has this got anything to do with Dad not contacting us yesterday?'

A faint smile played on Lance's lips. 'He's not here?' He looked from Ms Redman to Zeb, clearly trying to read their blank faces. His smile broadened. 'He's overspace, isn't he?'

His mother glared at Zeb. 'Go!'

Then Willis saw something he didn't think possible: Zeb crumpled. His face turned beetroot and he turned on his heel and stomped away.

Willis followed but slammed into him a few steps up the corridor. Zeb had recovered quickly. With a finger pressed to his lips, he gestured to Willis to remain silent.

Willis placed his mouth to Zeb's ear. 'Who's this Lance guy?'

Zeb gesticulated in the air, indicating he was at a loss. Together they listened to the words uttered at the front door.

'I need a place to crash.' Lance said. 'This place.'

Willis couldn't make out Ms Redman's words, they were muffled, but he could hear the fear in her tone.

'Ya gonna let me in?' Lance demanded.

Zeb turned to Willis. 'He's spinning out on Fast,' he whispered.

His mother said something. Something pleading.

'Ya gotta. I got nowhere else to go.' His voice sounded closer, as if he was inside now.

Abruptly Ms Redman came down the corridor and saw them. With a hand signal, she tried to shoo them away, back to Zeb's bedroom. Zeb remained in front of Willis and didn't budge. Scowling, she went to a closet and dragged out a load of bed linen. She shook her head at them and went back down the corridor. Setting Lance up in the living room, Willis guessed.

A door creaked and Willis turned in its direction, suddenly aware of another presence. Spud's round face peered from behind his bedroom door. He stared, wide-eyed. Zeb stepped past Willis, took the boy's small hand and led him back into his room. Willis stood at the door and watched as Zeb tucked him in and stroked him on the forehead.

Back in the bedroom, Willis didn't want to game up, he wanted to sleep. Zeb was disgusted.

Willis began undressing anyway and, to his surprise, Zeb followed suit. When he was in his pyjamas, he found his sleeping bag, rolled it out alongside Zeb's bed, and shrugged himself into it.

The night was cold against his face and the sleeping bag gave little warmth. Slow hours later and still awake, Willis heard a muffled, urgent voice from beyond their door.

'Stay away. I mean it.' Through his foggy consciousness, Willis vaguely recognised Zeb's mother's voice.

There was a long silence. Then Lance's voice barked out: 'C'mon, Marce.'

'I'll call the police.'

There was the sound of scuffling, then: 'Let go of me!' That was Zeb's mother. Willis imagined Lance's grabbing arms. His fists.

'Marce!'

'Go to hell, Lance Hack!' Her voice shook.

A door slammed and footsteps moved quickly away down the corridor.

'Well then schoff off!' Lance's shout came from the living room.

Willis waited. After a while, he heard Ms Redman's faint sobs through the wall. And whining. Who? It took him a second to realise it was Spud.

Turning, Willis looked through the darkness and up at Zeb's bed. As his eyes adjusted to the dark, he discerned Zeb's intense gaze. Directed at him. It was as if Zeb had been waiting for him to turn and look up.

'I'll just settle Spud,' Zeb said. He got out of bed and quietly left the room, leaving the door ajar. Willis listened to Zeb's soothing voice as he comforted his kid brother.

'It's okay,' Zeb murmured. 'That man'll be gone in the morning. And the next time we hear from our dad, it'll be to say he's coming home.'

Chapter 9

Zeb stood in a gloomy cave before a solid wooden door. A gleaming brilliance etched the cracks and outlined the door's four sides. Zeb was gaming alone – Willis had risen and left Zeb's place for school earlier, while Zeb pretended to remain asleep. It had been a very good plan. It gave Zeb a chance to game up without the burden of a noob getting in the way. Willis had certainly proven to be that.

He opened the door and let the light wash over him. Then stepped into thick jungle growth. As his eyes adjusted, the light receded from its initial dazzle and became no more than a soft glow. The click, whirr and buzz of hidden insects surrounded him. Soggy, warm air clung to his skin and stifled his breath. He turned and faced the other direction. As expected, the door he'd stepped through no longer existed. In its place sat an ancient tree with a gnarled, rotting trunk. He peered up at the dense sky. As he watched, clouds puffed into view and shaped into words.

Second EleMental: The Revenge of the Dinodroids

Zeb easily climbed the old tree and surveyed the game scenario from an upper branch. Behind him and close, tree branches swayed as if something lurched among them. He glimpsed a long yellow and green snout as it slowly stripped leaves, chewing them.

Caught by another sound, something faster, Zeb peered in the opposite direction and found a different story. Tree branches jerked forwards and whipped back, marking a line of crashing movement that headed directly towards Zeb's current position.

Two creatures – phenomenally large – were hidden under the jungle's canopy. One contentedly chewing foliage, the other tearing up the thick undergrowth.

Zeb clambered down and pushed through the brush, hurrying towards the first movement he'd seen. He could hear the second creature gaining on him, breaking into an even heavier run, as if it sensed Zeb was up to something.

Zeb burst into a small clearing and found himself running head-on towards a rotund dinosaur about the size of a single-decker ziptram. Its hairy, yellow and brown hide blended beautifully with the surrounding flora. The creature paused in its chewing and glanced up lazily. The stubby bronze horn above its tiny eyes glinted in the sun as it approached Zeb and sniffed at him with an inquisitive snout.

At the same moment, the second creature crashed into the opening and halted before them. Zeb leapt to one side, landed in a crouch and turned his gaze back to the first, watching to see how it reacted to the other creature's sudden appearance. In shock, he realised it had disappeared.

The second creature glared at him, steam wheezing and hissing from its flaring nostrils. This one was the size of a zipcar. Its head – while bulky and sporting a maw crammed with metal teeth – appeared small in comparison, its armoured body festooned in gunmetal plates that moved in mechanical rows along its neck and back. At its very end, but coming into view as the creature shifted about, swung a long tail bristling with steel spikes.

Without the presence of the first creature – where had it gone? – Zeb no longer had a plan. He regretted his impulsive decision to leave the relative safety of the tree.

'Attention, game,' he shouted. 'Weapon!'

'No weapons are available at this early point in the Second EleMental.'

'Why on earth not?'

'You haven't earned the points. No points. No weapons.'

'That's just great,' Zeb muttered. And was it his imagination or was the game voice sounding a little smug?

Through the corner of one eye, he detected the movement of a tree branch. 'There you are,' Zeb whispered, pleased.

He sprang in the direction of the movement, his arms stretched before him, fingers grasping. And thudded into the rough hide of the first creature, perfectly camouflaged against the jungle undergrowth about it. The creature hooted and shuddered, exposed where Zeb pushed at it. It seemed unable to maintain its camouflage and attempt to shake Zeb off at the same time. Zeb gripped its coarse hair and began climbing. The creature stamped wildly but Zeb clung on. He could now perceive its whole length and climbed to the crest of its jolting back. Clinging on, he twisted around until he spotted the other creature. It stood before them, keenly eyeing off the herbivorous dinosaur.

Zeb threw himself from the creature and ran for cover. Once hidden under some bushes, he turned and saw unmistakable panic in the eyes of the first creature. Its snout had retracted to a snub and a web of fine skin fanned out from behind its ears, pulsing with colours. He felt pity – it was an attractive display, but it was hardly frightening.

'Sorry, but better you than me,' Zeb said to himself softly.

The tank-like dinosaur moved in, snorting and wheezing, and lashed out with its spiked tail. The first creature hunkered down and managed to evade the attack, then lunged in with its horn – something more suited for digging roots, Zeb guessed. The enemy's tail swung back around and brushed aside the horn. Its deadly spikes ripped through the creature's web of skin, digging into its neck. The creature honked long and loud, a wailing siren of pain that echoed in the air. Zeb seized the opportunity, leapt to his feet and sprinted away.

'Score,' said the game voice, 'Zeb Redman: twenty; T-Wrecker: ten; Gigantus Veganraptor: zero.'

Good, Zeb thought, as he came to a halt in a scrap of grassland a safe distance away. Not many, but some points at last.

A roar cracked the sky.

He ducked under the cover of an overhanging branch at the edge of the grassland and searched overhead.

Three distant outlines cut through the air in military formation – jet-powered prehistoric birds of some kind. Zeb watched with glee, knowing they were a boss enemy that lurked at a higher level.

Abruptly, their roar ceased and the three pointed shapes froze in the air. Then the noise erupted again, but in reverse – a mashed, growling version of the original sound. And with it, the birds flew backwards, retracing their trajectories. At the same moment, the coarse grass beneath Zeb's feet began to tug from under him. And all about him, the jungle lurched into motion and slowly revolved, gaining pace until it became a spinning carousel with Zeb motionless at the hub. Everything whirled to a blur and shrank into a bright *pop!*

Zeb stood in his untidy bedroom.

'What's going on, Plush? I did not ask you to shut down the game.'

'A housecom has been activated. It's an overspace communication. You requested an immediate game shutdown in any such an event.'

'So I did. You go ahead and shut down too. I'll game up again later.' The tiny lights on the console faded.

He brushed himself off. 'Stalk mode,' he said to himself as if he was still in a game situation. He edged his door open without a sound. In the corridor, he could hear his mother murmuring down the housecom near the front door. He didn't like it; Lance could be listening.

It wasn't a long conversation and in no time there was silence. He waited but the silence remained. He crept back down the corridor, made a show of noisily opening and closing his bedroom door, then turned and marched towards the front door. He stopped when he reached his mother. She was sitting on the chair by the door, wearing her old dressing-gown, holding a tumbler of red wine in one hand and the lifeless housecom in the other. Her cheeks were damp.

'Someone call?' he asked.

She jumped at his voice, then put a finger to her lips and pointed at the glass sliding door that led to the living room. Only darkness lay beyond but Lance was in there somewhere, camped on the carpet. 'Not your father,' she whispered.

'Oh.' The disappointment was a slug in his gut.

'But it was about him.'

'Yeah? When's he coming home?' He didn't attempt to keep his voice down. 'Lance won't be pleased if—'

She waved him into silence, panic flashing across her face. 'They don't know when,' she said. Her voice was lower than ever. 'There's some spacefront disaster holding everything up.' She bowed her head and ran her fingers through her hair. 'Why'd he ever take that job? And he's working alongside that Space Guard crowd. All those miner disputes. He's in the thick of it. I knew he would be!'

Zeb wondered why she'd taken the call there, right by the living room door. It meant they were stuck muttering. But then he realised she'd wanted Lance to eavesdrop. She wanted him to know her husband was coming home soon. Only he wasn't. Her plan had failed and she was left here murmuring the bad news, hoping Lance wouldn't hear after all.

'Did you tell them about our freeloader?' he asked abruptly. He knew it was a silly question but he'd asked it in case Lance really was listening. His hate for the man twisted inside him.

'Quiet!' she hissed. She shook her head. 'They wouldn't care about that.'

Zeb raised a fist towards the living room door and glared at her. 'What kind of hold has he got over you?' he demanded. 'Explain that to me.'

She looked at the door without answering. Then she raised her tumbler to her lips and took a swallow. Zeb watched on.

'You must think I'm pathetic,' she said, wiping her lips dry.

'Of course I don't.'

She rolled her head away from him and looked down at herself. 'Look at me. I *am* pathetic.' She held her drink aloft and gazed at him. 'But don't worry. This is a temporary crutch. I'm in control of this. It's not in control of me.' She took a long swig.

In control? Zeb wanted to believe her. Wanted her to return to how she used to be. Pretty. Always laughing. Back when they were a proper family. Before his dad had lost his job, before his parents had started fighting. Before his dad had taken the job overspace – which had caused the biggest fight ever. It was only because his mum was scared, Zeb knew. But his dad had been so angry, insisting that he had to go, they needed the money. And so he had gone – just for a few months, he promised. Now, who knew when he was coming back – *if* he was coming back. Meanwhile, his mother wasn't coping, and there was this Lance Hack to deal with. Could he do something about that, somehow? He was the eldest son. His mother should be able to rely on him for support. Perhaps Zeb should stand up to Lance. Tell him he had to go. But deep down that idea frightened Zeb. Something told him such a confrontation would not turn out well.

'Anyway,' said his mother, 'why aren't you at school?'

* * *

Willis watched Zeb sneak in late to class and guessed he'd entered school through one of the blank security zones he'd shown such a gift for identifying. Zeb quietly made his way through the studistations and plonked down at his own, near the back, next to Arizona. Willis checked he'd managed to arrive unnoticed – yes, Ms Loveland remained bent over her master station, brow furrowed in concentration. When he turned back, Zeb sent him a quick nod, and rested his head on the desk of his studistation.

At recess, Willis followed Zeb to a lonely corner of the school quadrangle.

'You sleep like a rock,' Willis said. 'I couldn't wake you this morning.'

'I wasn't asleep. I just didn't want to get up.'

Willis was shocked by Zeb's frank dismissal of him. 'I was worried I'd be late for school.'

Zeb just shrugged.

Willis kicked the ground but forced himself to look back up and into Zeb's eyes. 'Did you gameplay? After I left?' He read the answer in Zeb's eyes. 'Only, I thought we were taking on the game together.'

'I couldn't wait that long. In fact, I've got some bad news. Mum says you can't come over anymore.'

Willis stared. 'But my Plush—'

'Just while that man's staying,' Zeb interrupted. 'Don't worry; I'll look after your Plush. After all, we're gamemates. Gamemates look out for each other, right?'

'*Gamemates?* But you're telling me we can't game together.'

'Only for the time being.'

Willis scratched his head. 'When's he leaving?'

'Dunno. And Mum doesn't want to ask.' He grimaced. 'My father would have a fit if he knew.'

Willis felt a surge of hope at that.

'But he's not gonna know any time soon,' Zeb added. 'Not with this mining dispute blocking all spacefront communication.'

Willis struggled for the right words. 'Zeb, I'm not sure how I feel—'

Zeb looked at him. 'You don't *really* mind me gaming on without you, do you? Your Plush is the only thing keeping me sane.'

Willis swallowed and said nothing.

Zeb beamed. 'There are all these cyborg dinosaurs. Wait till you play it.'

CHAPTER 10

Zeb arrived even later to school the next day. He looked as if he'd been gaming through the night. By mid-afternoon, he'd fallen into a deep slumber at his studistation. And this time it was obvious to all, even Ms Loveland. She stared down the length of the classroom from where she sat at the master station. Then she stood, straightened her tight, slate-grey skirt, and began walking towards him. But halfway there she seemed to think better of it – she stopped, sighed and signalled to Arizona.

'Arizona? Would you mind? Shake your neighbour awake.'

Then she returned to her master station.

Arizona left her station and approached Zeb hesitantly, standing over him with one arm partially extended. When she remained standing over Zeb, frozen, Willis got up and joined her at Zeb's side. Now the whole class watched, except Ms Loveland, who seemed to be making a determined effort not to.

Zeb had called Willis his gamemate. This was what gamemates did. Looked out for each other. Willis reached out and gently shook him. Zeb woke with a jolt and sat up straight. They watched him work through the daze in his head and finally peer at Willis while fighting heavy eyelids.

'What?' he said.

Willis whispered, not wanting all the onlookers to hear, 'I'm just making sure you're all right.'

Zeb's gaze wandered to Arizona and back again. 'What, both of you?' he sneered. "Course I'm all right.' He turned away and placed his head on the studistation desk again, closing his eyes.

Unsure what to do next, Willis looked to the front of the class. Ms Loveland had left her place and once more progressed halfway down the classroom. Her gaze was filled with concern.

After class Willis went to his locker, still brooding over Zeb's strange behaviour. He was reaching inside for his bag when he was hit by a putrid smell. He peered into his locker, then gaped in horror – stuffed within the tight compartment was the matted, bug-infested remains of a hound-like creature. Its half-eaten head sat at an angle that allowed its dead gaze to be level with Willis's eyes. Willis recognised it. It was the hound from *EleMental*.

Slamming the metal door closed, he staggered backwards and into the bank of lockers behind him. His locker door wobbled slightly ajar and he stared at it in disbelief then sniffed the air for confirmation. Oh hell, why'd he do that? The rank stench struck at him again and he gagged, his stomach churning.

'Hey, are you okay?'

He jerked his head around and took in the alarmed face of Arizona. She stepped forward into the alcove and reached out as if to touch him, then she checked herself and stepped back.

'I'm fine,' he managed. 'Just a little woozy.' Shock more like, he thought. 'From the smell.'

She sniffed the air. 'I can't smell anything.'

He inhaled carefully. Then took a deeper breath. 'No,' he said in surprise. 'Me neither.'

She smiled but was obviously confused. 'Well, if you're sure you're all right …' She started to move off. 'I'd better go.'

'Hang on.' Willis indicated his locker. 'Can I show you something?'

'Sure.'

She watched while he approached his locker with extreme caution. Standing back from it, he gripped the handle of an adjacent locker, raised his right leg and edged his locker door open with his extended foot. Then, straightening, cringing, he pointed to what lay inside.

His school bag.

It sat snugly within the compartment with room for little else, let alone the rotting corpse of a medium-sized animal.

He faced Arizona, his mind blank.

She raised an eyebrow. 'Very clever. Can I go now?'

That evening, when Zeb walked into his bedroom, he entered a primeval wilderness. It was all there. The heavy vegetation. The damp, sticky heat. The scurrying of hidden creatures. The shafts of light like giant Roman columns rising to cracks in the canopy. The biting smells.

But there was one problem. The Plush was off.

He clamped his eyes shut and wrapped his head in his arms. And when he warily looked up, he saw only his ordinary bedroom.

He dropped, trembling, to his bed. Stay zoomin, he told himself. Everything is okay. He lay on his bed and tucked his hands behind his head to steady them. He let his eyes drift closed again and tried to forget what he had seen. It made no sense. It couldn't have been.

But as he lay there something else in the room changed. Something subtle. He sensed it.

He kept his eyes shut, out of fear now. He stilled his breathing and reached out with his other senses. He wanted to know and he didn't want to know. Oh hell, was he in the jungle again? No, he wasn't – there was no heat. No random sounds of wildlife. But there was a new sound. It was as quiet as a breath.

And then he realised.

It *was* breathing he could hear. He was no longer alone. And the longer he kept his eyes shut, the harder it was to open them and the greater his fear. The seconds felt like dragging minutes.

He snapped his eyes open and gazed into the unshaven face of Lance.

Zeb swallowed back his alarm and remained motionless. Lance said nothing. He merely watched him.

Could he have been so distracted that he hadn't heard Lance enter? No way – his gaming practice had sharpened his wits no end. Yet Lance had done it. His stealthy entrance into Zeb's bedroom had been inhuman. Something one might only master after years and years of gaming practice. Lance was a miner from overspace.

So chances were he could be a Fasting gamefreak. And if that was the case, Zeb realised, he would have to re-evaluate what he thought about gamefreaks. Was it possible that, like the best gamers, they could have well-honed game skills too?

Lance was the first to break the tense stillness. He leant forward and pushed Zeb's legs aside, forcing Zeb to sit up on his bed. Lance parked himself next to Zeb and placed a large hand on his shoulder. It felt like a ziptram safety bar clamping down.

'We should talk,' Lance said.

Zeb stiffened under the strength of Lance's hand and was relieved when he removed it. 'Should we?' he asked.

'I want to get to know you.' He spoke slowly.

Zeb didn't respond.

'I suppose,' Lance continued, 'you think I've come all this way to visit your mother?'

'Who else?' Then the implication behind Lance's words sunk in. But that surely wasn't what he'd meant?

'Don't get me wrong,' Lance said. 'I have ...' he paused as if searching for the right word, '... feelings for your mother. But she's not why I'm here. She's ... an added bonus.'

A chill ran through Zeb. 'You can't mean me,' he said.

'Can't I?'

Zeb pulled further away from Lance and stared at

him, not bothering to hide his distaste. 'What have I got to do with you?'

Instead of answering, Lance considered something in silence. Then he sat forwards and directed his chin towards the floor. 'What's that?' he asked.

Zeb followed his line of vision but wasn't sure what had caught Lance's interest amid the strewn clothes, discarded Zeepad, various hyperboard bits and pieces ...

Lance pushed out with a slippered foot and exposed a dinner plate from under a pair of jeans. Old melted cheese had hardened along its edge and there was a trail of ants that could have been mistaken for a crack in the porcelain. Except it moved.

'That's just something leftover from the other day,' Zeb said. 'When I had a flashburger, probably. I'll clear it sometime.'

Lance rounded on him. 'You'll do it now.' He still spoke slowly and he emphasised each word, punching them out. There was warning in his face.

Zeb strove to keep his voice emotionless. 'I'll clear it when I want,' he said. Suddenly he felt furious. This stranger was living in their home, he was wearing his dad's slippers, and now he was coming on all heavy with him. 'You're not my father,' he said.

'I'm not your father?' Lance repeated and chuckled. Then he leant towards Zeb and narrowed his eyes. 'You must think life's one big skylark. You'll clear it in the morning, you say? Or not. Depending on how you feel at that particular moment, I expect. Well, I've got news for you: what you do ain't worth schoff. It doesn't count for nothing when it comes to the big picture. If you want to count, then you'd better start doing something that counts.' He looked at Zeb. 'Take me. Know what I do for a living?'

'You're a miner.'

'Aaah, got it in one. The toughest kind. I've mined in the asteroid belt. The belt of hell, we call it.' He sat back and gazed into nothing, seeing things Zeb couldn't. Something to do with asteroids, Zeb guessed. He wished the man were back on one right now.

'That's no cheap schoff,' Lance said. 'That's a real job.' He turned to Zeb. 'And what's your mum gone and married? Someone that's sunk to hobnobbing with Guard boys, no less.' He mimed spitting on the floor. 'Do you know what I was before I mined the guts out of spaceballs? A merchant spacer. Again, no schoff. A real job. Believe me when I tell you, I've mealed on more recycled schoff as a merchant spacer than you've flushed away in the toilet.' He grabbed Zeb's shoulder so tightly Zeb couldn't pull away. 'I only tell you this so you'll know for certain who you're talking to. When I say something, it's from the heart.'

Zeb believed him. He could see the fierce emotion in the man's eyes.

'And do you know what I was before that? An e-schooler. That's right. But I ran away to space when I was your age. I've spent more years farting around on moons and spaceballs than you've had gulping in oxygen back here on earth. To me, this planet's what's offworld. Somewhere to visit just to remind myself why I left.'

'I thought all the e-schoolers wound up killing themselves.'

Lance's palm shot up and Zeb flinched. But the blow never came – Lance let his hand fall and instead cradled his head in his hands.

'My childhood was … experimental.' He rolled his head, still holding it, his fingers trawling through his hair. It was as if he was attempting to get the right thought to drop into the right hole. 'It was all virtual school arenas, synchronous e-classes and listservs. That was my childhood.'

Zeb nodded. Ms Loveland had covered it in Social Comp. The e-school experiment, she'd called it. The government picked the so-called gifted kids and put them on 'the fast track to great things'. At the time, the media referred to them as *the connected generation*. Now history glibly called them *the disconnected*.

'These years you're living now,' Lance continued,

'they *should* be the best years of your life. Mine were stolen from me. I had nothing but … nothing but tech problems and squealing feedback. And isolation. Me and my *virtual* classmates.'

For the first time Zeb saw the weak man that sat next to him. He felt he should say something. 'I'm sorry,' he said. He spoke uncertainly. A murmur.

Lance froze but didn't answer.

Zeb should have remained silent, but instead he tried again. 'I said I'm—'

'I heard you,' Lance interrupted. His voice was ice. 'And I don't want the sympathy of some earthbound kid. And a novice gamer to boot.'

Zeb tensed. 'I'm no noob.'

Lance dropped his hands to his lap and sneered at Zeb. 'Oh yeah? Don't make the mistake of thinking I don't know about games. How do you think miners pass their time? The Spacefront Solution it's called where I come from. The Space Guard poured buckets into customising virtual games just for our diversion. Horrocore, v'hollies, veeporn – you name it. I'll be honest with you – I'm an honest man – we'd get Fasted to the eyeballs and go in hard gaming. Does that shock you? For days sometimes. And I was the best, no doubt about it.' He stared at his hands. 'I even knew the bloke who invented Plushes.'

'You did?' Zeb couldn't restrain the awe in his voice.

'Comet Mining Corps was onto his Plush like a shot. Them and their Space Guard buddies. He didn't only build the Plush console either. He was a genius at game design too. And out of everyone, he selected me to trial his ideas on.'

'Really? What was his name?'

'Grimwade Downer.'

'No way.' Zeb bit the inside of his lip. The names were so similar. Could it be the same man he and Willis saw on the ziptram?

Lance flashed him a look that showed he was thrown by Zeb's reaction. 'He was a brilliant man! And rumoured to be an e-schooler like myself. If so, then he was the only one of us who managed to get away unaffected. I'll never forget when he first came to the spaceball we were gutting. We all lined up but he barely glanced at the others. He just straight away pointed me out. I didn't even see him look at me. I'd just come from a bout of gaming, and I'd ingested quite a bit of Fast. It was just by luck he didn't see it in my eyes, I reckon. I spent a lot of time with him after that. He told me I accurately benchmarked miners' gameplay.' Lance tilted his head back, looking once more at far-off things in his mind. 'In his spare time, he'd blast away on a zip guitar. He called it his outlet. He'd sing these weird songs. And he had this odd way of saying things. Every genius has his mad side, I s'pose.'

'He must be filthy rich.'

'He would be if they could find him. He went out with the first batch of Plushes – piloting them with some miners on a far-flung spaceball. Apparently, when they shut down after one lengthy gaming session he just wasn't there in the room with them anymore. Gone! As if he'd stayed hanging around in gamespace. And he's been missing from the Corps ever since.' He laughed and shook his head. 'But it didn't worry me. I jumped straight into another cushy job. Comet Mining made me an offer I couldn't refuse. All I had to do was get my miner buddies to spend all their leave gaming. Stop them from ever wanting to blow their leave off a spaceball. Easy! There ain't nothing like Fasting with these new Plush consoles. They're made for it.' He grinned. 'Didn't know I was so important, did ya?'

'So why'd you come back earthside?'

His expression turned shifty. 'Let's just say I have my reasons. For one thing, Grimwade wanted me to. That's right, he never really disappeared. Not from me anyway. He joins me sometimes, when I'm gaming. Just turns up out of nowhere. Or speaks to me as if he's the game voice.' He gripped Zeb by the shoulder once more. 'I know what you're thinking – what a great life it must be mining. You get to game up all the time. And for free! But don't make the mistake of thinking it's all just Plushes up there.

When I said it was tough I meant it. Gutting spaceballs is the hardest life in history.' He thumped his chest with his other hand. 'And that's coming from one of the best asteroid gutters in the business. The belt's never known a miner like me. I've earned my miner's badges. *And* I've always been there for my mates. One way or another.'

Zeb was still wary of him, but hearing his words, he understood him more. Lance actually thought he was impressing him. The only thing that impressed Zeb was the fact that Lance felt the need to impress him. In one deft move, he yanked himself out from under Lance's grip. He stood up from the bed and stepped away from him.

'Where do you think you're going? I'm not done.'

'To sort the dishes,' Zeb said as he picked up the plate. 'I've decided to do it now after all.' He didn't dare look back as he walked out.

'Yeah?' Lance called after him. 'And just you make sure you do a good job.'

That same evening, Willis did something he knew his parents would not approve of. But once the idea had occurred to him, he couldn't put it out of his mind. After he closed his bedroom door, he pushed a chair hard against it and listened for a moment, one ear pressed flat to the door's surface. Silence. Good. Turning to his bag, he fished his Zeepad from it, dropped it into its docking station on his desk and faced his bedroom wall.

'eyeSPY.' He whispered the command word though he knew no one could hear him. He was taking no chances. Global search engines were great and had been around for longer than forever. But eyeSPY was another matter; eyeSPY was something the authorities had failed to close down. It was a GRE – a global ransack engine. The most powerful of its kind. eyeSPY scoured, rummaged, flushed and raked the world. The more personal, the better.

A two-dimensional image spread across the wall before Willis. Earth. It hung in space, its face lit by an unseen sun, placing Willis in the astral position of Venus, the ancient star of whispered confidences.

Willis gazed at the globe of shifting blues and greens and considered potential search strings. 'I spy: Arizona,' he began but then clamped his hand over his mouth. What more could he say? He didn't even know her surname. But the Earth spun before him, operating on his pathetic one-word search string. Horizontal white lines appeared over the image and proceeded to slice and hack. The dissected planet crumbled until all but one chunk remained. A section of North America with the state of Arizona positioned in the centre. Half of New Mexico to the right. California and the North Pacific Ocean to the left. And about a hundred billion tonnes of earth and rock hanging from beneath it in the shape of a mushroom stem.

Some search that was! Without her surname, *Arizona* would get him nowhere. He waved at it. 'Pull back,' he said.

Invisible hands returned the missing pieces, squashing everything together until the original image of a whole Earth hung before Willis once more. What could he say that was unique? Willis wondered. 'I spy: a *girl* named Arizona,' he said. And as an after thought, he chanced one more search clue: 'She rides a hyperboard.'

This time there were many more white lines and they razored through the Earth as easily as dicing an apple. The globe spun as thin slices fell away. And then it stopped. It had found something. No geographical chunk of America this time. But what? Willis couldn't fathom what he now peered at. A blue-green sheen like the ocean as seen from a jet. He flicked his gaze to the corner of the image where eyeSPY displayed some figures. 23-07-50. It was a date. Willis calculated – this had been recorded roughly four months ago. Three months before his family had settled in town. So, he was not looking at a live image relayed by the satellites. eyeSPY had dug up some past satellite capture – a piece of recent history. But he couldn't comprehend what it was.

In fact, though eyeSPY had hacked at the world until it had found something relevant to his search string, he seemed to be gazing at the blue-green globe of the world that had been present at the start of the search.

No, wait; there was something else. Willis tensed when he saw it. A face was reflected in the world, merged with the blue-green colours. It was indistinct but Willis could see that it wore a hyperboard helmet and was saying something, as if speaking to someone. As this was a recording from space, there was of course no sound – Willis could only guess at the words.

The blurry image of the face suddenly sharpened and Willis recognised it. Zeb!

Why was eyeSPY showing him Zeb's face superimposed onto the image of the world?

The face blanked out for a nanosecond like the click of an old-fashioned camera shutter. Or the blink of an eye. And with that, Willis's confusion cleared. He realised what he looked at.

As if eyeSPY knew it had been found out, it slowly pulled back and revealed surrounding images. Eyelashes. An eyebrow. Freckled skin. Willis had been looking at a membrane. The lens of a human eye. As the picture continued to widen, Zeb's face disappeared and

Willis gazed into the round face of Arizona. Arizona four months ago.

She laughed. The skin around her eyes and the edges of her mouth creased. Zeb had said something that made her laugh.

Willis sat down cross-legged on his bedroom floor and stared, mesmerised by the images that eyeSPY unfolded. Arizona wore a helmet too, and she and Zeb stood in a crowded place. Long grassy banks sloped in a cheerful midday sun. They were crowded with onlookers all facing in the same direction, towards a vast hyperboard park. Willis saw ramps, quarter-pipes, half-pipes, bowls, rails, steps and much more. Everything you could possibly want – if you were a master of the hyperboard.

It was a hyperboard tournament.

And Willis saw that Arizona had not been completely truthful about her hyperboard skills. She stood on her hyperboard at the tip of the highest ramp at the edge of the park. Zeb stood a short distance away, in a similar position. As if in response to a signal Willis couldn't hear, she leant forward and let her hyperboard drop. She plunged through the air atop her hyperboard, in complete freefall. Then the board's erupter – the small hard-laser generator fixed at the base – burst into life. She righted in the air and shot forwards horizontally, her arms out wide for balance. Willis watched her moves in awe. She crouched and rocketed onwards, sparking against rails and skirting the edge of one bowl then another. She leapt high, hugging her small feet to her as her board spun underneath. And somehow she connected with it again and bulleted on.

And then Zeb appeared at her side. And every trick she performed, Zeb matched with something special of his own. No one came close to them in skill – the other competitors that flashed by now and then seemed little more than a backdrop to their performance.

Willis marvelled at how well they worked together, setting up tricks for each other, close misses, last-minute ducks of the head as one of them flew over the other, synchronised patterns. The onlookers were on their feet, their hands raised high in applause. The magical atmosphere communicated what he couldn't hear: the clamour, the pounding music from the hovering speakers, the hyped barks of the commentator.

But something happened.

Though Zeb was far from Arizona, he sped in low towards her as she performed a spin. When she landed on her board, she shot towards him. At first Willis thought he was about to see a mock chicken dare, where one would pull out from the other's path at the final instant. But as they grew closer, Zeb veered slightly to one side. They still rocketed towards one another, but now would simply skim past on either side. Then Willis watched, astonished, as Zeb jumped high, flipping his hyperboard, and reached out with both arms towards Arizona. It happened swiftly and Willis almost missed what occured next – what Arizona did. Or, rather, what she failed to do. Instead of leaping to join Zeb in the extraordinary manoeuvre, panic leapt to her face. She dropped to a crouch and hugged her arms to herself.

Without Arizona there to counterbalance him, Zeb shot directly over her and sprawled onto the concrete of the hyperboard park. His hyperboard spun out of control, clattered to the hard surface, uprighted and drifted off aimlessly.

Arizona reeled off at an angle and away.

A man appeared from the side and rushed to Zeb, who remained face down and motionless on the ground. The man helped Zeb struggle to his feet and escorted him, limping, to the fence.

The competition continued for a while longer but Willis took little else in. Arizona performed no more tricks; her heart was clearly no longer in it. And when she stood on a podium clutching a trophy, he could see no triumph in her face. A male hyperboarder stood alongside her. In contrast to her, he raised his shining cup over his head and punched the air. But Willis knew the man was holding a trophy that should have been Zeb's.

'I'm not playing in this game, whatever it is.'

Arizona, 2050

LEVEL 2: GETTING HIGHER

CHAPTER 11

Zeb thrashed his way through thick undergrowth, pushed a branch aside and spied something in the distance: another door. This one stood in a small grassy meadow, hinged only to empty air. Words appeared suspended above it.

Second EleMental: The Revenge of the Dinodroids (save point)

The door opened with a small click, but what he saw through it disappointed him: the rest of the meadow. He stepped through anyway, but when he closed it behind him – *click* – the meadow disappeared. He stood in a square white room half the size of his bedroom.

'Well,' he muttered aloud when nothing else happened, 'either the game's glitching or this is one totally lamezoid cut scene.' Zeb drew a breath. 'Attention, game—'

There was a *ding*, the grinding sound of machinery kicking in and then a jolt beneath his feet. Zeb felt the sensation of rising. Fast.

'Never mind, game. Something's happening.'

The floor shuddered and the walls trembled. Then they cracked and fell away, abruptly exposing Zeb to a world in which he seemed to be perched atop a small mountain that was growing higher and higher by the second. Zeb dropped to the floor, crept to the edge where a wall had once been and looked down. The view stretched out on all sides as he rose. And it wasn't the jungle beneath him. It was a neighbourhood like the one where he lived. Zoomin, a hidden patch of gamespace! He made a mental note to return to it when he won the right to roam on free play.

Then Zeb looked closer, recognising streets and backyards. It was very like his neighbourhood Right down to the rusting zipcar wrecks that were permanently stacked one on top of the other in the overgrown back garden of the Woodheads' place. And there – the old-fashioned trampoline at the bottom of the Jacobs' garden. Zeb used to sneak in at night and bounce on it. And over there – the long row of poplar trees so tightly planted their stunted branches meshed. The row ran for several blocks and ended near his house. Remembering this, though one red-tiled roof looked the same as any other from this height, Zeb was able to pick out his own place. To confirm he was correct, he noted his father's blue zipcar parked outside their gate, just as it had been since he went overspace.

A movement caught his eye. To one side a tight herd of large, slender-necked dinosaurs trekked down the wide boulevard beyond his street – Saint Georges Road. The creatures were mechanoid. Their undulating necks had spiralling electric cabling that protruded like bulging varicose veins. They towered over the palm trees that lined the grassy median strip.

A smaller, tank-like creature bulldozed through a backyard fence from a laneway. The street was three up from his. That would make it Osborne Avenue, where Arizona lived. He sighted more of the creatures battling each other, probably in Arizona's very front yard.

Other creatures, two streets away again, amused themselves demolishing houses. Zeb watched as a heavy-duty dinosaur the size of a truck ploughed into the front of a house. The house was the largest in the street, which was doubtless why it had been targeted. The dinosaur disappeared as it smashed into the shuddering residence and re-emerged a moment later from the back. The house collapsed behind it.

Zeb wondered if the place had been Willis's. Probably.

And he spotted scampering, long-legged creatures with long, coiled antennas spiking from their ears. They toyed with moving zipcars that spun about and sped from them like panicked cockroaches. The creatures shrieked and pecked at the vehicles with sharp beaks. They were like seagulls at a picnic. One of the darting zipcars had the regulation yellow light flashing from it, indicating a learner was behind the wheel with an instructor alongside. Zeb remembered Willis mentioning his mother had a licence to teach. It might be her.

The accuracy of the depiction of his real neighbourhood – apart from the rampaging creatures, of course – was staggering. How was it possible? Plush games were meant to build images around you and trick your brain into believing they were real. This was something else again. The Plush – or the game, or something – seemed to be dragging personal perceptions from his mind and utilising them to enhance the game imagery. It certainly made things personal.

As the floor surged upwards, the streets and roads stretched into criss-crossed clusters and broadened further still into an endless web of bustling highways and ring roads. And it did not stop. The landscape expanded like a carpet rolling out in all directions at once, throwing up a massive, sprawling city that quickly shrank as he continued to rise, the view smoothing into rural browns, yellows and faded greens.

Spreadeagled on the floor, Zeb levered himself half over the edge and, with the wind whipping at him, carefully peered at the underside. What he saw stunned him. Fixed at the centre of the floor's base was a steel pole. That lone steel pole, rushing the platform ever upwards, was all that connected him to the distant earth below. He froze, suddenly aware of how tenuous his situation was.

As he crawled back from the edge, he gazed out across the sky. And that was when he saw the others. Countless platforms. All a good distance away but surrounding him. Like his, the platforms were connected to the earth by slender steel poles. Poles that, from this height and distance, were as fragile as dandelion stems. And on each platform clung a tiny figure. Their presence came as a shock. This was not some fancy scene backdrop made super effective on a Plush console. These distant figures were fellow gamers. Multiplay. But wasn't he playing solo? He hadn't plugged into the Plush Live network, he was sure of it. These days there was too much risk of that awful thing known as social networking. Yeuck. That wasn't his thing – serious gamers weren't into friendships; they were into winning. But here they all were. A zillion others. All playing co-op. No, not true. They were locked in separate parallel play. No one paid attention to anyone else. They fought to stay on their wobbling platforms. Some fell and hung clinging to the sides. Zeb watched their efforts to slowly lever themselves back onto their platforms.

And then one did pay attention to Zeb. Nearby, an older, squirrel-faced man was acting cocky. He stood close to the edge of his platform and jeered over at Zeb.

'Ha! Look at ya,' he shouted. He jiggled his arms. 'Ooh, too scared to stand up, are we?'

Zeb watched his expression change as his platform lurched one way and then another. With arms flailing, he slid along the surface backwards, teetered at the far edge and dropped over. By the time the wind currents carried his wail back up to where Zeb still lay flat on his stomach, it was a faint scrap of sound.

A far-off platform, close to the horizon, caught his attention. It was under attack. Flying creatures – from this distance the size of buzzing bluebottles – circled it, darting in and out. Better him than me, thought Zeb. He shook his head and turned away. He didn't want to see another figure falling. What was it with this game? First the cliff platform that led to the dragon's lair. Now a sky bristling with platforms! For a so-called first-person shooter, it sure was stuck on platforms.

Then Zeb hit cloud cover and everything disappeared in the compact fog. Zeb sucked in the damp air. Its chill bit his insides like swallowed lumps of ice. The platform shuddered, stopped and began to sway.

A sudden gust hit the platform, shaking it and throwing him sliding across its surface. The pole beneath groaned as the platform shifted. Then the platform swung back. With nothing to grip, Zeb slid headfirst the way he had come, scraping along on his stomach and clawing at the slippy, greasy surface with his fingers.

The platform veered and tilted again. Zeb pressed himself into the surface, imagining himself like glue. In the dense whiteness of the fog, he couldn't see where the platform ended and the open air began. Sight counted for nothing. Squinting, he calculated his position and decided he must be dangerously close to a corner. He rode the constantly swaying platform like a bucking horse, edging towards what he hoped was the centre – the point where the rocking should be the least.

'Attention, game. Am I there? Is this the centre?'

No answer.

This game gave no hints. He took in a deep, icy breath and in one fluid move leapt to his feet, splitting his legs wide, knees bent, like he was surfing a wave. With his eyes still shut, he felt the motion, second-guessing it and matching it with his own shifting weight.

Gradually the platform grew still beneath him. He remained frozen with his legs outstretched and his arms wide, and waited for the next shudder. It never came. Instead he sensed a warmth against his face. He opened his eyes.

The clouds had dissipated and he blinked into a wide blue slashed here and there with pillars of sunlight. All the other platforms were now gone. With a rush of pride, he found he stood where he'd envisioned, at the platform's dead centre. He remained poised in the clear sun a moment longer, his arms outstretched for balance. He felt superhuman.

'Score,' said the game voice at last. 'Zeb Redman: five points.'

'After all that?' Zeb shouted. 'Five lousy points?'

'Maybe you're not as good as you think you are.'

Zeb was amazed at the cheek of the game voice, but then the chime of a doorbell rang across the sky. He dropped his arms to his sides. 'Not again!'

Bleary from his long bout of gaming, Zeb trudged down the corridor into the entrance hall and opened the front door. He started in surprise when he saw who stood on the step, her arms folded: Ms Loveland. Even on a weekend she wore the same grey outfit. Hair pulled back. She was permanently the schoolteacher, it seemed.

'I haven't seen you at school lately,' she said, her expression flat.

Zeb squinted in the daylight that streamed in behind her. 'Isn't it the weekend?' he said.

'Today, yes. But not every day it isn't.' She sighed and shook her head. 'Once your work was exceptional, Zeb Redman. Where've you been these last few weeks?'

He glanced at the glass sliding door to the living room and put a finger to his lips for her to be quiet. 'I've been sick,' he whispered.

'Oh yes?' She didn't lower her voice. 'No one's told the school that.'

Zeb's gaze flicked again to the sliding door. Darkness lay on the other side of the glass but he knew Lance was in there. And he was the last person he wanted overhearing this conversation.

She pursed her lips. 'Is your mother home?'

Zeb shrugged.

'Can I come in? I'd like to speak to her. You too.'

Zeb wondered if his mother was up yet. Mid-morning? Unlikely. He stepped aside and let Ms Loveland in.

Chapter 12

The housecom beeped, announcing it had a caller, just as the door buzzed.

'Attention, housecom. Take a message,' Willis ordered, heading towards the door.

'The call is listed as urgent,' the housecom said.

'Who is it?'

'Zeb Redman.'

'Ha! Nothing for a week and suddenly it's urgent. Like I said, take a message.' Let him see what it's like to be ignored, thought Willis.

When he opened the door, the first thing he saw was the last thing he'd expected – his Plush console. Ms Loveland was holding it in both hands. Her smile was small and tight.

'Can you take this thing before I drop it? Your friend's done with it.'

Willis stepped forward and carefully took the console from her arms. 'I don't understand,' he said. He tried to maintain a blank expression but it wasn't easy. Though perplexed, he was also pleased to be getting his Plush back. He placed it on the carpet near his feet.

'Are either of your parents in? I think it's them I should be talking to.'

Willis instinctively stepped into the gap made by the open door, as if to block her entrance. 'Mum's working and Dad's ... They're both out. What did you want to talk to them about?'

She sighed. 'For one thing, why they thought it was okay for you to lend out that Plush.'

'They don't know.' When she stared, surprised, he added, 'Why should they? It's mine.'

Ms Loveland looked amazed at his words. 'Yours? Aren't these things incredibly expensive? Look, I don't make it my business to discuss the affairs of other students. But I'll tell you this: Zeb Redman is the most gifted student the school has ever known and something's going wrong.' She pointed to the Plush at Willis's feet. 'I believe it's connected to that.'

Willis looked down at it. 'He was okay about you giving it back to me?'

'Never mind about that.' She looked Willis over, as if coming to a decision. 'There's something else I want to say.'

Willis nodded, swallowing.

'You're a nice kid, Willis. *Zoomin*, to put it Zeb's way.'

Willis couldn't help but chuckle at that. It was weird to hear anyone else say *zoomin*; to hear Ms Loveland say it was positively bizarre.

'But in my opinion,' she continued, 'there's something wrong about the games you're playing. One in particular. *EleMental*, I think he called it. Where did you boys get it from?'

Willis decided to be vague. From the beginning, he'd felt there was something extra dodgy about the man named Grimble Dower, and Ms Loveland was the last person he wanted to discuss it with. She'd get all super-concerned. 'Nowhere in particular.'

'That's what he said. Well, I think it's affecting him. First, sleeping in class, and now not showing up to school at all. Is Zeb getting you into this stuff too? These weird games? I think he must be, if your results are any indication.'

'My results?'

'They're below expectation.'

Willis didn't know what to say. 'I really haven't been gaming that much.'

She studied his face. 'Well, something's going on. But perhaps my coming around here has shocked you enough. If you promise to cut down on these games, and if – and this is a big *if* – if I see an improvement in your results, I won't say anything to your parents. Deal?'

'Deal.'

She pointed to the Plush. 'Perhaps the two of you could play some educational games? They're supposed to be excellent.'

'I'd like that.' Willis meant it too. He smiled and she smiled back. But then her face grew serious.

'There was a man there. Not Zeb's father. Have you met him?'

Willis nodded.

'An uncle?'

'I don't know.'

'He appeared towards the end of my visit and actually wanted Zeb to keep the Plush. In fact, oddly enough, that's when Zeb finally agreed to let it go.' She turned to leave but hesitated. 'Just between us, I was beginning to fear we had a gamefreak on our hands. I'm no expert, but he seemed pretty muddled at times, the way gamefreaks are supposed to get. But then he handed the Plush over.' She shook her head, clearly puzzled, then with a sigh said goodbye and left.

Willis shut the door and leant against it, as if to make sure she didn't return. There and then, he resolved to study harder. Perhaps Zeb could help him? Ms Loveland had called him gifted! But she had also compared him to a gamefreak.

He stood with his back to the door a long time, looking down at his Plush. Eventually his dad's bespectacled face peered out from his office down the corridor.

'Who was that?' he asked.

Willis thanked his lucky stars that his dad had left it until now to investigate who'd been at the door.

'No one important.'

'Oh.' He pointed to the Plush on the floor near Willis. 'What's that doing there?'

Willis scrambled for an explanation. What he came up with was lame. 'I was just showing it to someone.'

His father looked astonished. 'Wouldn't it have been easier to bring *them* to it rather than *it* to them?'

'You're right. Silly me.'

'Well, better return it to your room. I don't have to remind you how pricey it was. You need to look after it.'

'I will. Sorry, Dad.'

His dad closed the door, returning to whatever he'd been doing.

Willis looked down at the Plush. Were those scratches? He bent down for a closer look. There was also a small dent on one side. He rubbed at the scratches. He guessed it didn't matter as long as it still worked. He picked it up and headed for his room.

'Attention, housecom,' he said. 'Transfer that last message to my Zeepad.'

In his bedroom he opened his Zeepad and hit a button. A frozen image of Zeb's face rose into the air over its screen.

'Start,' said Willis.

Zeb's face came to life.

'Hey, Willis, have you just told your housecom to take a message? I know what that means. Loveland's already there, isn't she? I wanted to warn you about her game plan. Do you know what she said?' Zeb put on a squeaky voice.

'He's out of control, Ms Redman. He can't stop himself, Ms Redman.'

Zeb dropped the put-on voice. 'And my mother just burst into tears. Loveland's got her really upset. Do you know she even hinted I could be leading you astray with these games?' Zeb's bodiless face began floating around the room. For all the world, it looked as if it was checking things out on the sly. Looking for the Plush. Trust even Zeb's housecom image to be nosy. 'By the time you turn this message on, you'll have your

Plush back,' the face said. 'But don't bother setting it up, okay? I'll be round first thing tomorrow.'

Willis didn't really want to talk to Zeb, so he sent a written message instead.

Zeb, don't bother coming round tomorrow. I'll be out all day. Ms Loveland's making things difficult. Been told to get down to my studies or she'll speak to my parents. Also, I have to keep the Plush here. Not for gaming, for study. Willis.

He switched his Zeepad off and began the task of reconfiguring his Plush for his room. It took a while – Zeb had made quite a few personal adjustments – but he didn't stop until he was done.

The next day, he rose before his parents were up. He used to go to the Floating Baths regularly before he met Zeb. Well, he was about to start going again. Besides, Arizona had mentioned seeing him there. Perhaps she went regularly too ...

CHAPTER 13

Willis clutched his baths bag and stood in the Floating Baths queue just before opening time. Though he was early, a good twenty people were ahead of him, including Arizona. A large group of boys jostled about just behind her, obviously keyed-up in readiness for a morning's reckless floatplay.

Willis pushed his hands into his pockets and watched Arizona from the corner of his eye, his head tilted down at an angle as if interested in something on the ground. He wondered if he should speak to her. She'd said he should. But how? Just walk up and say *Hi* and start talking? Then what? She'd probably think he was a complete idiot.

She wore light clothing. A yellow top and ruffled white skirt. He could see the outline of her bathers beneath.

As if she sensed his gaze, she turned to look at him. He hoped she didn't realise just how intently he'd been scrutinising her. He pulled a hand from a pocket and waved. Just a small wave – nothing so big and obvious that others, like the gang of boys, might see. She smiled in response, mouthed *Hello* and signalled to him to join her.

Willis wanted to badly but indicated the boys between them. No way did he want to risk skipping ahead of that lot.

Arizona nodded her understanding and seemed about to push backwards to him when the metal gates at the start of the queue yawned open and she was forced to file through.

Willis shuffled forward with the rest of the queue. When his turn came, he held his Zeepad to the gate monitor and entered the curved corridor that spiralled through the vast Floating Baths environment. He grinned when he found Arizona waiting for him slightly beyond the entry gate.

The corridor was essentially a clear giant tube that curved its way down to the floor of the Floating Baths. Willis glanced out through the wall of the tube as they weaved through the Bubble Arena, the centrepiece and main drawcard of any good Floating Baths. The arena surrounded them on all sides. With the floaters still changing into their bathers and otherwise getting ready, it was no more than a large empty space with giant, floating globs of wobbling water. Puffs of steam burst into the air at random intervals from the ceiling high above, maintaining the humidity. Wide patches of the tube's transparent surface fogged up from the steam, but quickly dissipated.

'Either you're following me or you're escaping Zeb,' Arizona said. Her tone was friendly but mocking.

Again she reminded Willis of Zeb. So forward.

'Why would I be escaping Zeb?' he managed.

'Zeb hates this place, and I reckon you know it too. And you know I come here. So which is it? Me? Or him?'

Willis was dumbfounded by her question and didn't answer.

The floating, trembling masses of water were now high over their heads. They reached the bottom of the tube and stepped into the cavernous Floating Baths compound.

She pointed ahead of her. 'I'm going this way,' she said.

He indicated the groundwater lanes. They lay in the other direction, in an out-of-the-way corner.

'You're going there? Okay. Well, enjoy your swim.' She walked off.

As Willis cut through the heated water his thoughts kept returning to the image of Zeb's face and his last words: *I'll be round first thing tomorrow.*

Willis reached the end of the lane, flipped over, and headed back. He stretched his arms further and swam faster.

As usual, the groundwater lanes were deserted. Most people hung out in or near the Bubble Arena. Even from this distance, the sound of the concentrated activity from the Bubble Arena was cacophonous. Willis knew if he swam at a steady pace, he could keep going for hours. But when he reached the other end, he glimpsed something that made him stop: the tall figure of Zeb emerged from the tubular entrance and peered about.

Willis kept low at the pool's edge and watched. Zeb stood out as the only one in the centre fully clothed. He wore the typical short jacket, gloves and sucker runners that marked out serious hyperboarders. He meandered towards the Bubble Arena, all the while gazing around and up at the floaters.

Beyond Zeb lay the large plunge pool designed for those who decided to drop from the air. A freshly painted yellow bridge arched across one corner of the pool and led to a group of tables and chairs on a patio. Willis spotted Ms Loveland sitting at one of the tables. Even though she was clearly visible in bright orange bathers, he didn't recognise her at first. For once, her blonde hair wasn't pulled back, and it frizzed out and down over her pale shoulders. It surprised Willis to see her hanging out at the Floating Baths. Especially in the patio section. It was such a teenagery thing to do, and she must be in her mid-twenties, at least. She sat with a large, hairy man around her own age.

Zeb marched to the centre of the bridge and gazed up at the boys who had been ahead of Willis in the queue. They larked about not far from the ceiling, rolling in and out of large, wobbling blobs of water, pushing them at each other. One boy broke from the group and slow-dived into the plunge pool. Another swooped low and looped under the bridge, passing beneath Zeb. He soared back into the air.

Zeb turned from them and stared at the serious floaters located even further away from Willis in the float lanes beyond the Bubble Arena. He craned his neck, examining each floater in turn as they coasted back and forth in dog-paddle style, appearing and disappearing through broiling clouds of steam, or clustered at either end, treading hot air and chatting.

A poolie floated over Zeb and eyed him closely. It was rare to see someone fully clothed on the bridge. Zeb ignored him and turned once more. Something had attracted his interest. Willis straightened in the pool and followed Zeb's line of vision. It was Arizona, in white bathers. She was sitting on the edge of a wooden bench on the other side of the plunge pool and chattering into her Zeepad. Near her, a lesson for toddlers was on the go. An instructor pushed tumbling infants through hoops. Arizona made room for a group of gleeful parents backing towards her and waving at the toddlers.

When Willis turned from the scene and back to Zeb, he found him staring right back. They locked eyes for grinding seconds. Then Zeb left the bridge and strode towards Willis, his face set. Willis felt sick watching him approach. He climbed from the pool and made for his bag on a nearby bench.

'I've been looking everywhere for you,' Zeb shouted before he'd even reached Willis. 'Off studying, eh? At the *Baths*? And you really are frightened of the Bubble Arena. No wonder you're a loser. In gaming and in life.'

Willis pulled a towel from his bag. He wrapped himself in it, took a deep breath and faced Zeb. 'I'm *not* a loser.'

Zeb seemed taken aback at Willis's directness. 'Okay, okay, whatever. But I've been looking for you. I went to that place this morning.'

Willis frowned, confused.

'Virtualitee,' Zeb explained. 'And guess what I found?'

'That weirdo in the sunglasses.'

'I found nothing!' He waved his arms in the empty air. 'Absolutely nothing. The address on the card says 2B. There's no 2B! There's a 2 and a 3, but nothing in between.'

'So it's all some con.'

'That's what I thought.' Zeb looked directly at Willis. 'Until I heard this.' He reached into his pocket, pulled out Grimble's singing card and held it up. The trumpets squealed out and the tiny Grimble appeared and sang at both of them, '*Come to Virtualitee and see for yourself. Indeedy yes. I went to—*'

'That old thing,' said Willis over the top of it.

'Keep listening. The words change in a second.'

Willis concentrated on the irritating voice.

'*Zeb went to Virtualitee but Zeb didn't see for himself. Yip, yip, yip. Zeb, Zeb, Zeb. Daylight's the wrong light. Night light's the right light … all right? To be virtually mine. Yip, yip, yip. Zeb, Zeb, Zeb.*'

Willis stared at it. 'It knows your name.'

'It sure does, doesn't it? And that's not all.' Zeb's eyes shone. 'The *EleMental* game even talks to me. I mean like *talks back*.' He put on a voice. '*No points. No weapons. Maybe you're not as good as you think you are.* It's like it's really Grimble. Right there.'

'That's pretty scary. What are you going to do?'

'What the card says, of course. Go at night.'

Willis shook his head. 'Zeb, that guy seriously freaks me out.'

Zeb laughed and waved the card. 'How could I refuse? I've got my own personalised invitation! And I'm already halfway through *EleMental*. Speaking of which, you've got to give me back the Plush. I mean it. A gamer never leaves a game unfinished.' He stepped closer to Willis. 'No one's confiscated it or anything?'

'Zeb, they say gamefreaks muddle reality and virtuality.'

'And you're telling me this why? I'm not a game-freak.'

Willis gritted his teeth. 'I can't give you the Plush. I need it for my study. To improve my scores.'

Zeb sneered. 'Don't you mean *marks*?' He stabbed a finger at Willis. 'Sounds like *you're* the one who's confusing real life and games.'

'I meant marks,' Willis said, 'and you know it.' His legs trembled as he spoke. He felt weak.

'Marks are easy.'

'For some,' Willis retorted. 'We're not all born geniuses.'

Zeb dismissed that with a flick of his hand. 'Are you my gamemate, Wil Boy?'

Willis nodded uncertainly.

Zeb always looked tall, but when he spoke his next words he seemed taller than ever. 'So prove it.' He balled his fists as Willis remained silent. 'I said *prove it*!'

He stepped closer. Willis wanted so much to take a step backwards but forced himself to stay where he was.

'Zeb,' he said, 'it's because you're my gamemate that I'm *not* doing this.'

Zeb held up his right fist and Willis flinched. Zeb seemed to be struggling with the urge to strike him.

'A gamemate who refuses to game up ain't no gamemate,' he said. 'You *are* a loser.' He spun on the spot and stormed off.

'Zeb!' Willis called out after him. 'Don't go there, Zeb.' Willis watched him stalk to the exit. He didn't look back.

'Willis? Are you okay?'

Willis turned. It was Ms Loveland, her towel around her hips, her wet hair in twisted tangles. The large man he'd seen her with stood a short distance behind.

She sighed. 'I'd hoped you two had sorted things out. I really thought you could be great friends.'

The man laughed and stepped forward. 'Belinda! Have you been putting this goody-goody and Zeb Redman together? I don't believe it.' He turned to Willis. 'Be careful of Zeb Redman, kid. He's a user.'

'Todd, that's not helpful.'

'Why not? It's true. Remember when he stole the prize money from that girl? What's her name? From the hyperboarding competition. It was all over the school.'

Ms Loveland glared at her companion.

'All right, I'm leaving.' He moved past Willis, heading towards the change rooms.

Willis remembered the hyperboard tournament he'd seen on eyeSPY. 'Did he mean Arizona?' he asked.

'I'm sorry,' Ms Loveland said. 'Unlike *him*,' she pointed in the direction Todd had taken, 'I don't go around repeating gossip.'

'He did mean Arizona,' Willis said. And at that moment, what small loyalty he still felt for Zeb melted away.

Chapter 14

Zeb stabbed at Willis's door buzzer and rapped repeatedly on the wood panelling. After a while Mr Jaxon opened the door and peered out.

'Willis in?' Zeb asked.

Mr Jaxon shook his head. 'He could be down at The Baths.'

'He has something of mine. I need to collect it.'

Mr Jaxon looked puzzled. 'What?'

'The Plush.'

'I don't think so. That was a birthday present. And he'd hardly be lending a Plush out.'

Zeb thought fast. 'I meant what's in it. I accidentally left my game in it.'

Mr Jaxon's face shifted from puzzlement to uncertainty.

'I know the way to his room.' Zeb squeezed through

the half-open door. 'I'll be quick.'

Mr Jaxon relented and asked Zeb to close the front door behind him when he left. He turned and disappeared into a room. Zeb opened Willis's bedroom door, paused, then closed it loudly. He tramped back down the corridor.

'I got it!' he called. 'Thanks, Mr Jaxon.'

No answer. Zoomin, he'd forgotten about Zeb already. Zeb opened the front door and – remaining inside – swung it closed with a big slam. Then he crept back to Willis's bedroom, softly closed the door, and loaded the game.

Zeb stood at the centre of the unstable platform and watched clouds in the shape of letters drift across the sky.

Second EleMental: The Revenge of the Dinodroids (save point)

A single puff of wind dissolved the words.

'Current score,' said the game voice, 'a trifling five points.'

'All right, game, don't rub it in.'

'Rub it in? It was merely a summary of your feeble performance to date.'

Zeb rolled his eyes. What was *with* this game?

Keeping to the centre, he shuffled in a circle and surveyed the gamespace. He found something new. Suspended in the air a short distance from the platform hung another door, massive and vault-like – a colossal block of metal in the sky. Its smooth surface glimmered. The door to the Third EleMental. It had to be.

He edged to the rim of the trembling platform and let it tilt forwards until it sloped towards the door. He curled his toes tightly around the rim and leaned in until he touched it, creating an arch over the bottomless divide between him and the door. He ran his fingertips across its chilly smoothness. Nothing suggested a keyhole. No hidden nick for a secret unlocking system. He pushed harder. Nothing. He pushed as hard as he dared – still it didn't budge – then used the momentum to return safely to the platform.

Backing up to the platform's centre, he stared at the blank door and thought through his options. Zero. How the hell was he supposed to get through?

He motioned with his hands like a magician. 'Open!'

Nothing happened. Of course.

A strong gust whipped up and almost knocked

him from the platform. He sensed this was a central challenge. The game meant to fling him from the platform one way or another. He had to get past the door before it did that.

In the distance, he spied a tiny, black shape flying towards him. He could now detect its distant droning. He stared again at the door. How could he open it? Think!

The shape grew quickly, separating into three distinct shapes. Sharp. Jet-like. Their droning growing to a roar. Zeb remembered his glimpse of them at an earlier level.

'Open sesame!'

Nothing.

'Abracadabra!'

Nothing.

The flying shapes were almost upon him. He could see them clearly now. They looked like pterodactyls with sharp-angled metal wings. Jet engines fixed beneath each wing spat fire into the air.

'Alakhazam!' he shouted at the door.

Nothing.

'Hocus pocus!'

Nothing.

'Simsellabim!'

Nothing.

The first of the prehistoric bird droids raced in with a piercing shrill. Zeb threw himself flat as it whammed over him, trying to knock him off the platform.

'Score,' chirped the game voice. 'Zeb: ten; technodactyls: minus ten.'

Zeb grinned. A score at last! And *technodactyls*. Now there was a name and a half.

A cracking sound split the air. Zeb swung around in time to see the platform's surface near his hand blister and puncture. The second of the technodactyls rocketed past – close enough for Zeb to glimpse its arsenal: rows of thick-barrelled guns rotating on each of its wings. Bullets continued to blurt from the guns' heavy muzzles, zinging in the air beyond the platform and the door.

The third technodactyl thundered in immediately behind the second. Zeb tumbled to the platform's far edge as its wing-guns erupted. The platform shook and heaved as bullets stabbed the surface he'd just occupied, shredding it. He gazed up in renewed wonder at the Plush's capabilities as the creature's immense underbelly boomed overhead.

'Score – Zeb: twenty; technodactyls: minus twenty.'

The platform made for an appalling defence position. Perhaps he should just slip off and free-fall away? Call up a parachute at the last moment. If the game would let him, that is – this game didn't seem that charitable. The idea of exploring other areas of the gamespace was tempting. He could come back here another time.

No. He'd never fled a battle before. He had to see it through.

The droning of the technodactyls' engines altered as they banked and came around.

There was a groan, and directly beneath Zeb's feet a portion of the platform gave way, taking Zeb with it. He threw himself onto what remained of the platform as the shattered piece plummeted earthwards. The platform lurched and tilted sharply and he held out his arms to steady himself. Inching backwards, he reached down and ripped up a jagged fragment. Then he hurled the fragment at the door. It clattered against it and dropped away out of sight.

Nothing.

'Open, damn it!'

Nothing.

Behind him, the roar of the technodactyls mounted. They'd regrouped and were returning.

'Score to date,' said the game voice. 'Zeb: ten; technodactyls: minus twenty.'

'Hey, I was twenty before!'

'Ten points have been deducted. You're taking too long.'

Zeb shook his head, almost stumbled, checked his balance and turned to the giant door in the air.

'Fee fi fo fum!'

Nothing.

But there was a change of a different kind. No drone of engines. He swivelled his head around. The technodactyls were gone. Instead there was a whistle in the wind. Soft but growing. Where was it coming from? Then he looked up and saw them. They were directly overhead and high above. They'd cut their engines and, in precise formation, free-fell towards him. As they carved through the air, the whistling from the tips of their wings grew in intensity until it became a whistling chorus. Together, the three creatures opened fire.

As the bullets ripped into the remains of the wobbling platform, Zeb danced – he capered, careened and cavorted, performing a wild dervish that took him to a slide on his knees, a spin on his back, a roll of his body and a whirl back to his feet, pirouetting over blistering, shredding, detonating surfaces.

The technodactyls dropped past on three sides, disappearing below him, and the windy silence returned. Zeb crept to the edge and gazed over. Directly beneath him the technodactyls still plummeted earthwards. Then abruptly their engines erupted into life and they wrenched themselves from their free-fall, pulling themselves upwards through the air in tight formation.

'Score – Zeb: twenty; technodactyls: minus thirty.'

Breathless from the attack, Zeb watched, impressed, as with a howl of engines the three technodactyls rose high once more. They rocketed upwards, broke pattern and spread out like a blossoming firework. They were getting cocky. How could he capitalise on that?

An idea struck him.

He watched them regroup in the distance, forming a close triangle. He sensed they were coming in for the kill; they'd done with fooling around.

Zeb positioned himself with the door behind him, and faced them.

They came in fast, the hungry roar of their engines thrumming through his bones.

Wait, he told himself.

The barrels of their wing-guns moved up and down as they targeted him, checking and rechecking. The fat chambers behind the barrels rotated. Bullets locking in, Zeb guessed.

Keep waiting.

Their beaks were long and pointed, crammed with teeth like broken glass across a factory wall.

Wait.

Their eyes flicked. Glinted.

Wait.

The one at the head of the formation let loose with a piercing squawk. A battle cry?

Almost there.

Forget the door, he willed them. See only me. Your defenceless prey.

Now!

Their wing-guns blazed.

But Zeb no longer stood there. He'd stepped backwards off the platform. Flinging his arms up, he seized at the platform's jagged edge and clung on. Over his head, bullets smacked into the door.

Zeb craned his head backwards and studied the door's surface. Nothing. They'd glanced off with no effect.

But that wasn't his plan anyway.

The first of the creatures slammed into the door and disintegrated.

That was his plan.

Zeb swung wildly as the flaming debris cascaded about him, almost crashing into him as it dropped earthwards. Gripping firmly, he strained backwards and again studied the door.

At the centre was a faint crack.

He swung himself deep under the platform for the greater protection he realised he needed. As the platform was now little more than a jagged wedge of scaffolding, it was possible to hook his feet in, one into a fracture and the other against the edge. He could see the remaining two technodactyls through cracks in the platform. They came in hard, their engines grinding in reverse and emitting wailing shrieks as if crying out *Too late! Too late!* Side by side, guns erupting, they powered into the door. Zeb clung flat to the juddering platform's underside as the air exploded with shattering debris.

After long seconds of airborne chaos, there came at last a stillness and the sighing breath of the wind. Zeb unhooked his feet. Twisting around on his aching arms, he peered over one shoulder to view the result.

Success! A growing network of cracks mapped outwards from the centre of the door. The cracks joined and thickened until the surface began to crumble. Then, with one final, aching shudder, the steel door gave way. As if first discharging from within, shattered fragments the size of fists blasted from the door, spinning and banging against Zeb's back and head. Zeb clung to the platform, his head down, his eyes squeezed tight and his teeth gritted against the dust that blanketed him.

Gradually things settled into quiet. He opened his eyes and watched the final pieces falling far below. He resisted the sudden urge to clap his hands in victory.

'Score!' said the game voice. 'Zeb: a lot. Let's think about this. Ten, plus twenty for each defeated creature, that's seventy, plus – how about a bonus fifty? Why not! One hundred and ten in total. Technodactyls – er, let me see: minus one hundred and twenty! Technodactyls defeated. Gone, gone, gone. Dead, departed and dismissed from the mind.'

Zeb dragged himself onto the platform and lay on his back. Only then did he have the energy to talk. '*From the mind?* Just what kind of a game are you?'

'You have talent, Zeb Redman. Indeed you do. I look forward to more of your gameplay.'

'Are you something else the Plush does? Are you some kind of built-in something or other?'

'Indeed I am. Yes, no, maybe. Are you ready for the Third EleMental, Zeb Redman?'

Zeb remembered what Lance had told him about the Plush inventor named Grimwade Downer and how he'd stayed behind in gamespace and sometimes spoke to Lance as a game voice. It had to be the same man. 'No game has ever talked to me this way before,' Zeb called. 'It's as if you're there. Not just a voice. Are you Grimble Dower, once known as Grimwade Downer?'

He was answered with silence.

'Hey? You still there?'

Still no answer.

'Go then. Like I really wanna know.'

Zeb climbed to his feet and rubbed the dust from his hair. Something then grabbed his attention. Where the door had hung there now lay a ragged hole in the air. Its edges glimmered silver and gold. He peered closer, carefully keeping his balance. Through the hole, he saw a horizontal bar. It glinted in the sun, connected to nothing. Zeb smiled. He loved these things! Defeating the last battle had unlocked a hidden reward.

Leaning backwards on the last jittery piece of platform, he braced himself, leapt across, caught hold of the bar, and swung into the air beyond it. As he arced high, he caught sight of a giant, spiralling waterslide.

He shot through the entryway and spun into the transparent tubing, an umbilical joyride that wound its long way to Earth. Twisting into a streamlined posture, Zeb bulleted downwards.

'Hello, world!' he cried. 'I'm coming right atcha!'

When Zeb shot out of the joyride, he hung in the air and gazed down at the rows of groundwater lanes and floating swimmers. I know this place! he thought. The Floating Baths. And not just any suburban Floating Baths, the very ones he'd visited earlier that day. And he saw something else that stunned him. It wasn't just the place that was identical. The people were too. There sat Arizona in her white bathers. And over there his teacher, Ms Loveland. She sat with the year coordinator, a total dead loss. Todd the Sod everyone called him.

How could any of this be?

And then he spotted Willis, doing laps in one of the groundwater lanes off to the side. Watching him, Zeb knew immediately who Willis was in this Third EleMental. The number-one boss enemy.

CHAPTER 15

When Willis opened his bedroom door, he stepped into the Floating Baths. He stopped just inside the door and gaped at the sight – the layout was identical to the place he'd just come from, where he'd ended up spending his whole day. There, too, were the same people. He recognised the form of Ms Loveland some distance away. She dived from a board and floated into the air. Willis stared at her in horror. Her face was twisted in menace. Todd followed her, bouncing off the board and breaststroking through the air. His face, too, was an uglier representation of its true self, filled with malice.

Zeb was gameplaying in his bedroom. *EleMental*. It was the only explanation Willis could come up with. And somehow, the game had the ability to conjure up distortions of real people.

Pushing back his fear, he searched the surroundings. 'Zeb!' he yelled. 'Where are you?'

A splashing to his left caught his attention and he spied a fight between two figures in the groundwater lanes. Zeb! It had to be. Willis ran to the edge. Yes, Zeb fought with somebody – or something. His enemy had his back to Willis, but he could see Zeb's determined face clearly. It was not distorted like the others. It was the real Zeb.

'Zeb!' Willis bellowed again.

Distracted, Zeb glanced in Willis's direction. His combatant seized the opportunity, leaping up and pushing Zeb under. That was when Willis saw what – *who* – Zeb battled. It was himself: Willis. And like the others, it was evil. White eyes were set deep into muddy grey skin. It was as if his own face had merged with an eel's. The Willis creature held Zeb under water, sneering. And when it brought Zeb – gasping and coughing – to the surface, it spoke. 'You lose, gamefreak,' it said.

Zeb losing? The words were almost as unfathomable as the entire scenario.

Zeb screamed as the creature lifted him by the neck and shook him. It wasn't a gaming scream, something perhaps born of an unexpected thrill. It was a scream of genuine pain.

The distorted figures of Ms Loveland and Todd now stood at the edge of the groundwater lanes. They plunged in and began streaking through the water towards Zeb.

'Attention, Plush,' Willis cried.

'Plush here,' said the calm female Plush voice.

'This is Willis. Shut down the game. Now.'

'You are not at a save point.'

'I don't care. *Now*, please.'

Everything folded, tornadoing into a dense, bright dot. *Pop!* Only he and Zeb remained in Willis's bedroom. Zeb sat in a corner, staring wildly and breathing hard.

'Zeb, what's going on?' Willis said, going over to him. 'That was too real. And I was in it!'

Zeb's breathing slowed. He looked up. And then he sprang at Willis, hammering his fists into him. Willis buckled under the blows but Zeb didn't let up. Fists, knees, feet, Willis felt them all crash down on him.

Willis whimpered. 'Zeb,' he pleaded. 'It's me, stop.' He could hear how weak he sounded and felt ashamed. And then, deep within him, he felt the first stirrings of anger. Zeb's pummelling went on without mercy. And Willis felt his anger grow into rage until he didn't care about the blows his one-time gamemate rained down on him. What he cared about was fighting back, defending himself. Slowly, he pushed himself up, grimacing against Zeb's violence. The strength from his rage rushed through his body. He flung his arms out, hurling Zeb from him. Startled, Zeb fell back but then jumped up quickly and threw himself at Willis again.

This time Willis feinted, blocked with one arm and slammed a fist into Zeb's face.

'I said *stop*!' Willis shouted. He lay into Zeb hard, in tears, delivering precision strikes for all the reckless hits he'd received. Zeb fell backwards, stunned. 'It's me, *Willis*, your gamemate,' Willis said in rhythm with his heavy punches. 'Remember me? Remember me?' When at last Willis pulled away, gasping, he glowered at Zeb's huddled form.

Zeb raised his head and gazed up. His face was bloody. His lips moved silently.

'What?' Willis said. 'I can't hear you.'

Zeb's response was a weak utterance: 'Sc ... Sc ... Sc ...'

'*Score*?' said Willis in disbelief. 'Is that what you're saying?'

'Score,' Zeb said, now louder. And he struggled to his feet, trembling, his eyes fixed on Willis. He looked ready to begin the fight all over again. 'Attention, game,' he called, looking into the air. 'Score.'

'Zeb,' Willis said, 'I've shut the game down. The Plush too.'

Zeb glared. 'I don't believe you. The *real* Willis could never fight like that.' He thrust forwards, knocking Willis to the floor. In the time it took for him to recover, Zeb had already opened the bedroom window and scrambled through.

Willis climbed to his feet and stared after the receding figure of Zeb running into the night.

There was a rap on his bedroom door. His mother entered as Willis rubbed his sore ribs.

'Willis! What's going on in here? What was that shouting?'

'Sorry, Mum. The Plush. I forgot to seal the room for sound.'

'I thought I heard your friend Zeb?'

Willis shrugged, then winced as pain fingered through his body. He hoped she didn't notice. 'You must've misheard.'

She looked puzzled. 'It sounded quite violent. You know I don't want you playing violent games.'

'The violence was ... unexpected. It was a demo Zeb got from somewhere. I'll give it back.'

She nodded and sat down on his bed. 'Is everything all right?'

'Sure.'

She patted the bed and Willis obediently sat down beside her. His body ached but he pushed the pain from his mind and let her take his hands in hers.

'You've not seen much of me lately,' she said, 'because of my new job. And Dad's been distracted with trying to get his consultancy business up and running. I'm sorry if we haven't given you the attention you need.'

Willis said nothing. With everything going on in his own life, he hadn't really noticed the goings-on of his parents. They had their lives and he had his. And sometimes he told them things and sometimes he didn't.

'Being a teenager isn't always easy,' she continued. 'I understand that. It's a time of growing independence and responsibility. But if you ever need to come to me for advice, promise me you will. We're here for you. Never forget that.'

'Okay, Mum. No problem.'

She let his hands go and put her arms about him. A groan of pain escaped from Willis. What would she make of that? Rising emotion? How embarrassing. 'I love you both, Mum,' he said quickly as a cover-up.

She squeezed him tightly and Willis fought back more gasps. Then she released him and stared at the window. 'Wil, why is your window open?'

Willis lay back slowly on his bed. 'Ah, I'm not feeling

a hundred per cent. I thought some fresh air might help.'

She felt his brow for a moment. 'You seem all right. But close the window, it's freezing in here.'

After she left, Willis lowered his head into his hands. Alone with his aches and his thoughts. He thought about his mother's words. *We're here for you.* And then he thought about Zeb. Who did he have?

Chapter 16

To Willis's amazement, Zeb showed up to school the next day. Late, of course. He sauntered in, plonked himself in front of his studistation and sat motionless, looking neither right nor left. When he began quietly murmuring during free study time, Willis did his best to ignore him. The other students did likewise. But when the low sounds continued, Willis's mounting curiosity eventually dragged his gaze over. Zeb was rocking gently in his chair and clutching his head.

Ms Loveland sat at the front of the class, bent over her own station, oblivious to this new development in Zeb. But that changed when the murmuring stopped and the hollering began.

'Attention, game,' Zeb cried.

Everyone turned.

Zeb stood before his studistation, determination

plastered across his face. 'Weapons!'

He turned and gazed in Willis's direction – though not *at* him, Willis realised; Zeb was gazing *through* him. Willis followed his line of sight but saw only the rest of the classroom. He turned back and found Zeb scrutinising the rest of the room, as if calculating the lie of the land. Then he threw back his head, let loose a war cry and leapt at his studistation, punching, kneeing and kicking at it.

Nearby students jumped from their own stations and backed away. Ms Loveland rose with the remainder of the class. But she stayed at the front, gaping at Zeb. Only Willis left his studistation and moved closer.

And that was when his vision shifted.

As if phantom fingers had passed through his skull and thrown a switch, he now saw what Zeb saw: a creature the size of a zipcar and with the appearance of a metallic armadillo. Dark, liquid eyes watched from above a snout that blew and snorted. Beneath the creature's belly were two parallel rows of heavy wheels set within wide conveyor tracks. The creature whirled, shifted and spun on these tracks. In place of limbs, stumpy, grey metal cannons jerked up and down – to no avail, as Zeb rode atop the creature, higher than its weapons could reach. There seemed to be nothing the creature could do to fling him off.

'Attention, game!' shouted Zeb. 'Where's my weapon?' Miraculously, a small dagger appeared in his hands. Zeb gawked at it. 'You're as bad as my old Magnum.' He hung on tight to the angry creature, attempting to plunge the dagger into one of its eyes.

Willis glanced at the other students. They watched Zeb with amusement. They did not seem shocked like he was. Arizona, standing at the very back of the class, caught Willis's gaze. *Why?* she mouthed.

'*Why?* Can't you see it?' Willis called. He pointed to the menacing creature. It didn't make sense. There was a game happening and yet no Plush was running. There was no way of shutting things down.

When he took a step closer to Zeb, the classroom disappeared altogether. He stood in a dense jungle wilderness.

Zeb glanced at him from the crest of the whining, shuddering creature. 'Wil Boy! You're just in time. I've unlocked a hidden level. Call up a weapon. I could do with some help.'

Willis was astonished at how easily Zeb had forgotten their last, violent encounter. 'Zeb,' he said, 'none of this is real.'

'What? 'Course it's not.'

Willis shook his head. 'No, it's not even a proper game. There's no Plush operating things. You're in class and everyone's watching you.'

Confusion darkened Zeb's expression for a moment. The creature took advantage of his distraction and shuddered wildly, throwing Zeb to the ground. Screeching and reversing, it bore its twin cannons down on him. Red lights set along their sides flickered and a thick sound grew, like a jet powering itself.

Willis caught the shape of something else. For a blink, the creature seemed transparent and he glimpsed something inside it. Willis stared harder and saw it again: the shadowy outline of Zeb's studistation within the creature's gut exposed like something in an old-fashioned X-ray.

Then the creature's cannons detonated.

Zeb, being the expert gamer he was, had already predicted the creature's move and dodged and rolled out of the way. Willis jumped out of the way too, and hunched over, clasping his hands to his ears against the deafening roar. Trees on either side blew apart as Willis staggered backwards. And the jungle around him disappeared. Once more, he stood in the classroom, surrounded by studistations and students. Here the two missiles exploded into the classroom's back wall and shards of brick erupted and rained down on him. Thick dust enveloped the room.

As the dust settled, Willis stared in horror at the broken bodies of his classmates scattered in the rubble. He recognised a scrap of burnt pink in the debris and remembered Arizona had been wearing pink that day. There was no sign of Zeb. He could see the creature though. It engaged its gears with a harsh whirr and click, and advanced onto the rubble, shifting left and right as if searching for Zeb.

Zeb sprang from behind a pile of rubble and bounded at the creature with his dagger held high, clearly intent on a counterattack.

The creature shrieked as Zeb landed on top of it, hitting down hard with his feet and stabbing at it with his dagger. 'I have you now!' he yelled. His ecstatic, high-pitched scream hit the air. And with a violent, downwards jab with his dagger, Zeb pierced one of the creature's eyes. Black liquid spurted from the eyeball with a yielding *pop* and the creature howled in pain, reversing wildly. Zeb leapt off and heaved at one side of the creature, groaning with the effort. The creature tilted on its side, rocked, and slammed back to the floor when Zeb let go. Zeb tried again, shouting and kicking.

Willis turned to where the back wall had been

blasted away, leaving only chaos and death. Shaking his head, he stared at the horrific scene until his mind ached. Then, before his eyes, the mash of corpses and rubble dissolved, leaving only the polished school floor. The wall reintegrated like a slo-mo backwards explosion. And there stood Arizona again, by her station. She watched Zeb in dismay. Not a dust mote on her.

Willis gazed in the same direction and, straining his vision, saw once more the outline of Zeb's studistation within the creature. The studistation's shape grew in clarity until Willis stared at what he knew Arizona and everyone else watched: Zeb atop his motionless studistation, jabbing at it with a metal ruler, then rocking it from side to side. Willis and the other students looked on as Zeb fought with the piece of inanimate school furniture. Biting it. Scratching it. Punching it.

Willis took one step towards Zeb and the scene shifted back to the jungle. Zeb clung to the side of the thrashing creature as it ploughed through the undergrowth.

'Zeb, stop!' Willis cried.

Zeb turned at the sound of his voice and with a roar the creature flung him wide. Zeb fell, crashing, losing his dagger.

'Attention game! New weapon.'

'No new weapons available,' said a game voice. Male. 'You'll just have to make do, gamefreak.'

Willis couldn't believe what he'd just heard.

'What kind of first-person shooter is so tight with its weapons?' Zeb snarled. He scrambled to his feet as the creature bore down on him, attempting to grind him under its tracks. Zeb tumbled aside, glancing at Willis. 'I'm losing!' he shouted. 'Help me!' When Willis failed to move, anger flashed across Zeb's face. He shook his head. 'Some gamemate.' He turned and ran into the undergrowth, disappearing.

The creature clacked and whirred as it followed in pursuit.

Willis squeezed his eyes shut and concentrated on a remembered image of the classroom. And when he opened his eyes, that was what he saw. Zeb's studistation sat motionless before him. Zeb himself was gone.

Ms Loveland was also gone, no doubt looking for assistance.

The students around Willis chattered with excitement. Willis ignored them and approached Arizona.

'Where'd he go?' He spoke in a whisper though there was no need.

She looked surprised and pointed at the door. 'He

ran out, totally hysterical. Don't tell me you didn't see? You were standing right there. The closest.'

Willis shook his head. 'I didn't see.' He tried to understand what he *had* seen. 'I saw something else.'

'What kind of game is this?'

Willis, 2050

LEVEL 3: GOING DOWN

Chapter 17

The next morning Willis rose early and sent a note from his Zeepad to the kitchen's message board. *Gone to the library to study*, it flashed. He had a late start at school, so his parents might find that surprising, but not unbelievable. It was the kind of thing he sometimes did. Once. He departed without breakfast, unsure where he was really going. But when he kicked his hyperboard into life, he wasn't surprised to find he turned left and headed towards Zeb's house.

He was shocked, however, by the sight that greeted him.

Zeb's mother sat slumped on the kerb outside her house. She was wearing her faded pink dressing-gown, the same one she had on when he first met her. Behind her, smoke rose from one side of the house. Three police tanks were parked haphazardly across the pavement, blue and orange lights blazing from their roof racks. The scene was strangely quiet, as if he'd arrived immediately after a devastating storm. People moved about purposefully and spoke in hushed tones. Two men busied themselves setting up a series of poles. A searing red beam shot out between the poles, connecting them and effectively cordoning off the Redman house.

Uniformed police waved people on. Willis picked up his hyperboard and moved to the far side of the house, then turned around. From this perspective he could see that an entire front corner of the timber home was missing. The wooden beams closest to the devastation were charred and smouldering. The nearby side fence had also been flattened and still burnt in places. A man wearing a bright yellow helmet stood next to the gaping hole, nodding and talking to a woman with a microphone. A third person stood back slightly, operating a zipcam.

Willis peered through the hole. A small movement in the shadows caught his eye – Zeb's peeling poster stuck to a wall. The guitarist swung his instrument back and forth like an executioner's axe. Willis realised he was looking at what remained of Zeb's small bedroom, almost unrecognisable in the rubble. Men in bulky outfits and heavy yellow helmets moved about the ruins of the bedroom, inspecting and recording.

Two uniformed women stood near one of the armoured police tanks, their helmets by their feet. One spoke on a com; the other crouched next to Spud. Though she talked to him, Willis saw the boy wasn't responding. He kept looking in the direction of his mother. Then he turned and stared at Willis. The woman tracked Spud's gaze and studied Willis for a moment before she turned away.

Willis made his way over to Zeb's mother. The men who had set up the poles had just reached her position on the kerb and they included her in the cordon without speaking to her. Willis ducked under the light beam and approached her. Her face looked swollen and she shivered.

'I came to see how Zeb was,' he said nervously. Now that he was close, he saw dried blood caked under her nose. Her eyes and cheeks were damp. One eye was half-closed in a shadow of grey and blue.

'Zeb?' she said. 'So he's not with you, then.' She spoke as if she first had to locate each word separately in her head.

Willis shook his head and felt a rush of relief. Her question meant Zeb wasn't lying in the rubble of his bedroom. He was someplace else. Alive.

Ms Redman began to cry. 'Zeb didn't come home until

late last night,' she said. 'Heaven only knows what he'd been doing. At first, I was relieved to see him. Lance ...' She whispered the man's name as if frightened he lurked nearby. 'Lance was ...' She broke off again.

Willis crouched next to her. Uncertain what to do, he touched her arm. She immediately placed a hand over his without looking at him, holding his hand there.

'Lance straightaway turned on him,' she continued. 'He told him – he told Zeb he was his father.'

Willis stared at her, hardly comprehending.

'Zeb went ... insane. The way he suddenly fought back.' She dropped her head and tears dripped into her lap. She didn't speak for long seconds. 'I don't think he knew where he was. And now he's disappeared somewhere. Lance after him.'

'Lance is Zeb's dad?'

She wiped her eyes. 'Or Andrew. I don't know what's true anymore. Lance might be his father. That's why I ended up letting him stay for ... for too long.'

She looked into Willis's eyes and gripped his hand.

'If Andrew were here, none of this would've happened. His place is here. I need to tell him what's happened but offworld messages aren't getting through. I should never have agreed to him going overspace. The money was never worth it, and anyway, it's totally irrelevant now. Look what's happened.'

Willis glanced at the smouldering house and tried to think of a way to ask what *had* actually happened. But then a voice called from somewhere: 'Mother!' It was young and distressed. Willis spotted Spud running towards them. A policewoman followed a few steps behind.

Ms Redman pulled away from Willis and called out. 'Sanderson!' Spud rushed into her arms. She repeated his name as she held him, crying and stroking the back of his head.

Willis climbed to his feet and moved off. The policewoman eyed him and approached. 'Friend of the boy who ran away?'

Willis nodded. 'Is he in trouble?'

'We're concerned for his wellbeing. Do you know where he's gone?' Before Willis could answer the com-badge on her shoulder strap buzzed. 'Sir?' she said into the empty air.

Willis couldn't hear the voice at the other end and guessed she had an implant.

'I have a friend of Zeb Redman's here. There could be intel.' There was a moment of silence. 'Uh-huh, uh-huh.' She turned back to Willis. 'So where's he gone?'

'I don't know. Can't you eyeSPY him?'

She sighed with impatience. 'I will ask the questions.

But for your information, don't think we haven't tried all world-based search engines, including GREs. It's a first line of detection.' She paused. 'Your parents happy with you eyeSPYing on others, are they?'

Her sudden shift in gear caught him off guard. 'I don't eyeSPY on others,' he said, collecting himself. 'I just thought you might be able to find him that way.'

'Well, we can't. And if you're really a friend, you should be able to name some places we can check.'

Willis brought a hand up to his chin and rubbed it. 'I'd have to think about it.'

She glared at him. 'Well, think hard, young man.' Willis felt like a suspect. She turned from him and spoke into the air again. 'He doesn't know anything … Okay … Uh-huh. Out.'

'Can you tell me what happened?' Willis ventured.

'No. You'll have to find out some other way. On the news, maybe.' She turned to go but then hesitated. 'How close are you really?'

'Zeb and I are gamemates. Well, we *were*.'

She flipped open her Zeepad and studied it. 'There is something you might be able to help with.' She scratched her head as if trying to make sense of what was on the screen. 'The boy, Zeb Redman – his mother reports that he kept yelling for a weapon. And calling out the word *score*.'

Willis dropped his head. He felt numb. Her words didn't surprise him but he so much didn't want to hear them.

She leant in close to his face. 'You *do* know something, don't you? What is it? Tell me. He could be in grave danger.'

'How?'

When she said nothing for a moment, Willis wondered if his question had angered her even more. But then she nodded slowly, as if reaching a decision. 'All right,' she said, 'I'll explain something. And when I'm done, I want you to spit out whatever it is you know. Your friend and a man named Lance Hack were involved in a violent exchange. This man Lance Hack is a dangerous criminal.' She flicked open her Zeepad and looked at the screen. 'There was an incident on a Comet Mining asteroid. It seems he was a regular game-hitter, ingesting heavy doses of Fast. Without any warning, he turned on his fellow miners with something called a rockshocker. His actions resulted in the deaths of fifteen of his colleagues and numerous injuries.'

'Oh God.' Willis could barely take it all in.

'Know what a rockshocker is? It's a piece of heavy-duty asteroid-blasting equipment that has no business being earthside.' She nodded towards the smouldering corner of the house. 'It did that. And it's our belief that he's out to get your friend for some reason. Wherever they've gone, they're beyond eyeSPY. Which doesn't make sense either because they can't be off planet. We'd know if Hack tried that. And the fact that we can't get a fix on *either* of them, even though there is plenty of footage of them straight after the explosion, is too much of a coincidence. It supports our belief they're both in the same place. Somewhere beyond satellite detection. Hack most likely in pursuit of Zeb. If he hasn't caught him already.'

Willis gazed at her in shock.

'But where? That's the question.' She looked at Willis meaningfully.

He stared back.

She clicked her tongue. 'Well?' she asked.

'I'm sorry?'

'Spit it out. Both Hack and your *gamemate* are missing. What can you tell me?'

Willis swallowed. 'Zeb could be a gamefreak.' As the words came out, he felt like a traitor. 'Maybe,' he added, in an effort to soften them.

She didn't look surprised. 'Is he seeing things that aren't there?'

Willis swallowed. It felt like he was putting the knife in. 'Yes.'

'That's called *gameblur*. The game kicking in any time. Comes from consuming Fast while game hitting. The numbers are growing. Damned if we can find out how kids are getting hold of Fast. It doesn't make sense.'

Willis shook his head vigorously. 'He wasn't Fasting.'

'You just said he was a gamefreak.'

Willis told her about *EleMental*, trying to keep it simple. 'It's all coming from this one demo game,' he finished. 'I'm sure of it.'

The police officer seemed to be only half listening. She held up a palm to indicate she'd heard enough. 'Fast has to be in there somewhere,' she said. She slapped her com. 'Sir?' she said into the air. 'I do have some intel. The boy's a full-blown gamefreak. We should check all local gaming points.' She turned back to Willis. 'Any we should start with?'

Willis nodded. 'Screamers,' he said. 'And a place called Virtualitee.' He spelt it for her and wondered if he should tell her how Zeb couldn't find it during the day.

She conducted a conversation with her com-badge for some time and listened to responses only she could hear. Willis waited.

'Zeb Redman should be treated with caution. Looks

like we have two out-of-control gamefreaks on our hands.' She was about to say something else when her head turned sharply, as if a third person had cut in on the conversation. 'What? Yes? Uh-huh, I see.' She turned back to Willis. 'They say there's no such place as Virtualitee – with a *y* or two *e*s.'

'It's new. We only just found out about it ourselves. It's only open at night.'

She looked curious. 'Who told you about it?'

'A weird guy in black sunnies. And he doesn't always seem … in focus.' As soon as he'd said them Willis regretted his last words.

She stepped closer and stared into his eyes. 'You Fasting too?'

Her question stung and he felt intimidated by her proximity. He swallowed. 'I told you,' he said. 'It's not Fast.'

She shook her head slowly, then slapped her com-badge. 'Are you there?' she said into the air. 'Downgrade that last intel I just sent through. The source is unreliable.' She dismissed Willis with a wave of her hand and proceeded back to the house.

The full meaning of her last words hit him like a slap on the face: she thought he was a gamefreak too. 'It's not Fast!' he called after her.

If she heard him, she didn't show it.

Chapter 18

Willis's hyperboard slapped against his thigh as he stamped down the street. The slapping pained him. And he let it. He didn't throw his hyperboard to the ground and use it. His anger choked him and the pain helped keep it in check.

He'd branded Zeb as a gamefreak. Now the police thought Zeb was spinning out on Fast.

He let his hyperboard bash his leg harder, trying to smack away the thoughts.

'Willis!'

He ignored the cry of his name.

And the man who had pushed his way into Zeb's house – maybe his father! – was after Zeb with a rockshocker.

'Willis!' He heard his name again, then there was the *thrum* of a hyperboard's erupter. 'Willis, wait!'

Arizona overtook him on her hyperboard and curved,

snaking in on him and blocking him. 'Willis! Hold up!'

'No, I have to study.' He spoke louder than he'd meant to and continued more quietly. 'And you should too. All of us – it's all any of us should ever do. Study, study, study.'

'I've just boarded past Zeb's place and—'

'I know. I've come from there.'

'And you're off to study?' She back-kicked her hyperboard into silence and stepped off. 'Willis, what's got into you?'

'He's on the run. Zeb's on the run.' Willis watched his words sink in.

'From the police?' she asked.

'No, from some crazed man his mother knows. The police are trying to help Zeb. I think I know where he's gone – but when I tried to tell them they wouldn't listen.'

Arizona frowned. 'Then *we've* got to help him.'

Willis dropped his head. 'He's beyond our help.'

She looked perplexed. 'What's got into you? You two are gamemates.'

He sighed. 'We've not been seeing eye to eye. You've seen how he's become – the police are calling him a gamefreak.'

'Which means he needs our help more than ever.'

He gazed into her eyes. 'After what he's done to you?'

It was her turn to sigh. 'You're talking about that stolen money story, aren't you?'

She spoke in an accusing tone and Willis felt ashamed he'd mentioned it, though he didn't know why he should.

'It was just something someone said,' he admitted.

'You want the real story? I gave the money to him! He talked me into entering a hyperboard comp. Freestyle. And right in the middle of the finals group he went into a flip trick that meant picking me up and spinning me.'

Arizona paused, clearly seeing it all happening again before her eyes. Willis could see it too.

Zeb and Arizona racing towards each other, leaning forwards on their hyperboards.

The spectators on their feet.

Zeb reaching out to her.

Arizona recoiling, dropping into a crouch, wrapping her arms around herself.

Zeb tumbling through the air.

Falling hard on his face.

His riderless hyperboard. Drifting in one direction then another.

'What was I supposed to do?' she cried suddenly. 'It wasn't something we'd planned. He took me by surprise. I … I hate being touched. I pulled away and did my own thing. He totally stacked. I won my section. He got eliminated. So later I forced my prize money onto him out of guilt. It wasn't a huge amount but it was pretty good. I made him take it all. End of story.' She raked her fingers through her hair, looking away from Willis. Then she looked back. 'Only it's not the end of the story, is it? He chucked in hyperboarding and bought a secondhand Magnum with the money. So maybe he's a gamefreak because of me.'

Willis felt stupid. He'd believed Ms Loveland's idiot boyfriend.

Arizona fixed him with an intense stare. 'So are we going to help or not?'

He wanted to nod, but said instead, 'I'm frightened. It's not what the police think. There's this game. And this place. Remember when Zeb smashed up his studistation? It's because he thought he was in a game. The policewoman said it was called gameblur and it's brought on by Fast. But I could see it too! And I know I'm not doing Fast. It's got to be something to do with this place.'

'So what do we do?'

Willis dropped his hyperboard to the ground, jumped on and kick-started it. Then he looked at her. 'Find it. I've no idea where it is. But I know where we can start looking.'

Chapter 19

Willis's parents weren't home when Arizona and Willis got there. They went straight to Willis's room, and he turned on the Plush.

'Ari, if this game's turning people into gamefreaks, you don't want to be exposed,' he said. 'Stand with your back to the wall. You'll be on the perimeter and the Plush will automatically exclude you from the game.'

Arizona agreed and backed up to the wall. Willis turned to the console and instructed the Plush to start up the game which was still inside.

No title flew across the room and bounced off the walls. No crash of music ushered in an opening scene. No credits announced the producers and artists. There was only darkness and stillness.

Willis stood waiting.

A setting gradually unfolded about him, starting with the audio. The familiar, echoing cacophony of human activity always present at the Floating Baths faded in. And then the sights, shaping from the darkness. Willis stared around in renewed amazement, remembering his earlier exposure to the replicated Floating Baths, when Zeb had stolen into his bedroom. He moved forward and surveyed the scene, the game level Zeb had been playing – had been losing. Over on the benches, an instructor addressed a small group of toddlers wrapped in animal-shaped rubber rings. Near the ceiling, floating boys clowned around.

Willis peered across to the patio on the other side. Yes, he could make out Ms Loveland in her bright orange bathers, sitting with Todd.

At last, translucent words rose dripping from the water and hung among the floating swimmers.

Third EleMental: Eelements

Arizona appeared beside him. 'Willis, it didn't work. I'm in.'

Willis reached out to touch her for reassurance then remembered what she'd told him and let his hand drop. 'I don't get it,' he said. 'The Plush should have excluded you.'

He watched her gaze around in awe, as he had just done. 'It's all so familiar – but so strange,' she murmured.

'Let's be quick and get the Plush to shut it back down.'

She nodded in agreement. 'I'm with you.'

'Attention, game,' Willis called. 'We need some information.'

'Who's that kernocking at my door?' There was no doubting that the game voice was Grimble's, just as Zeb had described. As mad as ever.

'Willis Jaxon.'

'Indeed? The Plush owner. And I see you have yourself a female companion.'

'What?'

Arizona said, 'I think he means me.'

Willis started with the sudden realisation of what Grimble's words implied. He could see them! This wasn't a game with a voice like Grimble's. It *was* Grimble. It was as if he actually stood somewhere beyond the game, watching them. He turned to Arizona. Her face was serious, her gaze filled with concentration.

'My name's Arizona,' she announced, 'not *female companion.*'

'Indeed?' said the omnipotent voice of Grimble. 'What a delight. Come, both of you. Come to Virtualitee and see for yourself.' Willis recognised the tinny whack and crackle of electric strings as the invisible Grimble bashed at a guitar. 'Ooh indeedy,' he croaked.

'Fine,' Willis snapped. 'So where is it?'

There was a long silence.

'Hey, I said where is it?'

But he was gone, had moved on to more pressing matters perhaps. Annoying people in other games, maybe.

'Willis, look.' Arizona walked over to a wall and pointed at a cluttered noticeboard.

Willis joined her and scanned the many leaflets and notices advertising gym classes and lesson times. 'It's an old-fashioned noticeboard. What of it?'

'There!' She pointed to one corner.

Willis saw it. A singing card was pinned there. 'Well spotted.'

He pulled it from the board and peered at it. A little Grimble figure danced and squeaked: '*Come to Virtualitee and see for yourself. Yip, yip, yippy.*'

The card tingled in his fingers. 'It was just sitting here. Like a clue in a game puzzle. Waiting to be found.' He flipped it over. On the back was a map with names. A red X lay over one narrow street.

Arizona looked over his shoulder at the card. 'There it is,' she murmured in his ear. 'Virtualitee. In the middle of the city. Degraves Street. It looks more like a laneway.'

A sudden splash grabbed their attention and they tensed. The sound of splashing at the Floating Baths was not an unfamiliar thing – but this was different. Immediately Willis became aware of the otherwise stark silence of their surroundings. The familiar cacophony had died away unnoticed.

They slowly turned to face the main Bubble Arena behind them. It was deserted, the globs of water hanging lifeless like dead amoebas. Willis glanced at the groundwater lanes. A broad ripple extended across its surface.

'We should turn this game off now,' he whispered.

'Good idea,' Arizona agreed.

But then they came. They rose from the empty groundwater lanes as if they'd clung to the pool's bed all along, preparing for this dramatic emergence. And their manner of rising was inhuman. They grinned as they rose stiffly from the water, their arms and legs still. All the people he'd seen at the real Floating Baths were replicated here. No. Willis gasped. More than that. His mum and dad also stood in the group. As he watched, the group began to transform, distorting the images of the people they replicated. Their skin turned an oily, muddy grey, their mouths lipless, their teeth jagged. Their eyes shrank to pinheads.

As one they advanced across the surface of the water, stepped from the pool and onto the wet floor.

Willis saw himself at their head – the sneering version of himself Zeb had been battling. The malformed creature locked eyes with Willis and a look of malicious glee spread across its face.

'Do something!' Arizona cried in Willis's ear.

The Willis creature sprang into a run, shrieking and baring its ridges of sharp teeth. The others sprinted behind, racing across the wet floor towards Willis and Arizona.

'Attention, Plush,' Arizona shouted. 'End game!'

The furthermost part of the gamespace began to revolve, ripping up the Floating Baths piece by piece. It swelled into an elongated tornado, wheeling level and consuming everything. Groundwater lanes, wooden benches, plunge pool, patio, Bubble Arena, all coiling into its revolutions. And it roared forwards, sucking in the back line of the racing crowd of creatures. They howled as they were sucked up, eaten alive. Ms Loveland. Todd. Willis's parents. The lead creature, the evil caricature of Willis, glanced back at the tornado then sped faster, pouncing. Willis and Arizona clung to each other as it shot through the air at them, its claws extended.

Then it froze in mid-air.

And simply hung there.

Suspended.

The creature swivelled around and peered down its length.

And howled.

The tornado had reached its feet but remained poised, whirling yet not progressing forwards – something Willis had not seen before in a game folding. It was as if it possessed a consciousness and toyed with the creature. Rippling tendrils emerged from the mass of the tornado and licked at the creature's webbed toes. The creature struggled to break free, yammering and snarling. The tornado crept forward, swallowing the creature's feet and its bony ankles, creeping up its thighs, dragging the agonised creature into itself. And suddenly the Willis creature broke into a spin and stretched. The tornado grew into a thick spot of light, a spinning luminescence.

It hung in the air before Willis and Arizona, as if eyeing them for a moment.

Then – *pop!* – it disappeared.

Arizona still clung to Willis, which was amazing. Hadn't she said she hated to be touched? He gazed around his bedroom in confusion.

'It's not supposed to be that way,' he gasped. 'None of it is how real games behave. Throwing distorted images of yourself at you. That's unheard of. It's all this Grimble guy – he's doing something.' He faced Arizona. 'And I thought only I could control my Plush and tell it to shut down the game. After I caught Zeb gaming in my bedroom, that's how I set it up.'

She stepped back from him and took his hands in hers. 'Lucky for you, it turns out I can too.'

He nodded. 'And with the words *end game*! They're not even command words Zeb and I set for this Plush.'

'Aren't they? They were the first words I could think of.'

He allowed himself a deep breath. 'I'm sorry about what happened – I just froze. It was strange, seeing myself like that. And my parents.' His words came hesitantly; his thoughts were elsewhere: with her hands, holding his. They were warm and calming. 'My mind went blank,' he added after a few seconds. He fell into a silence, mystified by her touch.

She tilted her head and studied him, as if trying to figure out his thoughts. She leant in closer.

Without thinking about what he was doing, he leant in and met her.

They kissed quietly. And for that moment, there was just the two of them. No Plush gaming. No gameblur. No mysterious Virtualitee. No Zeb. No problems.

He could taste her sweetness. He didn't want to forget that taste for as long as he lived.

'C'mon,' she murmured when they drew back. 'We've got the address. Let's find the place. Maybe things will make sense then.'

They collected their hyperboards at the front door and left the house holding hands.

'Maybe we could simply find Virtualitee and get back to the police about it,' he said, his mind still focused on her touch.

Arizona agreed. 'I know exactly where it is. It's close.'

'Meanwhile, I'd like to see you try a three-sixty on that hyperboard.'

She smiled. 'You're on.'

She did more than that; in fact, more than Willis had thought humanly possible, proving that winning the hyperboard competition had been no accident. In one quick move, she kicked her hyperboard into life and spun into the manoeuvre. As she pirouetted one way, her hyperboard spun the other, once, twice, three times, and on, four, five, six. The hyperboard's erupter raged and the suspension lasers dazzled his eyes.

He watched awestruck as she lightly landed on her board, in perfect balance, and shot down the drive. She hit the road strip reserved for hyperboards at full tilt, and sped away without looking back.

Willis dropped his hyperboard down with a clatter, jumped on, checked his balance, and sped after her.

'What the hell was that?' he called as he caught up and came alongside her.

She beamed. 'A twenty-one-sixty popshoveit with body varial. Er, I think.'

She laughed and surged ahead before he could utter any more words of amazement.

Willis accelerated after her.

Chapter 20

They found Degraves Street easily – though why it was called a street was anybody's guess. It was little more than a slice of space between two red-brick buildings. A vacated Separate-While-U-Wait divorce bureau stood on one side, a dusty Nothing-Over-A-Grand discount store on the other.

Willis and Arizona entered the narrow street hesitantly, hyperboards tucked under their arms like shields. The dirty brick walls rose high on either side of them. Willis could make out small windows close to the top. They were caked in dust. Windows with no purpose. Windows never looked through. They reminded Willis of the blank stares of a gamefreak.

'Shouldn't we be right through to the other side of the block by now?' Willis's voice shook. He kenw they'd walked further into the gloom than was possible.

Arizona pointed ahead. 'This must be the place.'

Willis exhaled in surprise. Where there had a moment before been only darkness, there now stood a single door. An old-fashioned fluorescent sign crackled and buzzed over it. With some letters dead, it flashed *Vi tu l* in the murkiness. At the foot of the door lay a grubby mat with *Welcome* burnt into it.

Arizona touched his hand and spoke in a hushed tone. 'Not quite what I expected.'

Willis pressed a finger to his lips. The door was ajar and voices drifted out. He caught a voice he recognised.

'Do you hear that?' he whispered.

She nodded without a word.

It was Zeb's voice.

Arizona held Willis's arm and they walked cautiously into the store's mustiness. The interior was in keeping with the outside. Tiny. But as Willis's eyes adjusted, he saw it went back a long way. And everywhere he turned, he saw battered cardboard boxes – mountains of them piled recklessly one on top of the other. And all bore the same words: *Plush – Budget Version.* Cheap plastic signs on chains hung randomly from the ceiling over the boxes: *Get 'em now!*; *Out they go!*; *They're virtually walking out the door!*

A single passage led through the piles of boxes to a dilapidated counter. And there, leaning at the counter with his back to them, stood Zeb. Willis's old gamemate slowly turned and faced them. 'So,' he scowled, 'you've come to Virtualitee to see for yourself? *And* brought your sweetheart.'

'Zeb, I—' Willis began, but words escaped him.

Zeb's eyes were bright and alert, a million miles from how he'd appeared the last time Willis saw him. Zeb spread his arms wide. 'Isn't this something? Plushes everywhere! And each with a bonus game thrown in.'

'Let me guess,' said Willis. '*EleMental.*'

Zeb grinned. 'That's right. So, no need to sneak into your place anymore. And there's no need to pretend we're gamemates.'

'Zeb, we're worried about you.'

Zeb sneered. '*We?*'

Willis turned to Arizona. 'Ari and I.' He was surprised when she didn't back him up. She stood motionless, her face without expression. 'The police too,' Willis continued. 'And your mother.'

'Yeah? Well forget it, I'm staying here.' He pointed to the entrance. 'So now you can go. Tell my mother and anyone else who cares they can all leave me alone.'

'Did you know Lance is after you? He's wanted for murder.'

Zeb threw his head back and barked a laugh He

glanced to his right. 'Did you hear that? You're a murderer.'

From behind a stack of boxes on the counter Lance emerged. A heavy rockshocker hung from his shoulder. He looked at Willis. 'I thought this boy wasn't your friend anymore?'

'He's not, Father.'

'Why're you calling him *Father*?' Willis said and lurched forwards, seizing Zeb's arm. 'This isn't right. You've got to come with us.'

Lance swung the rockshocker around. The massive barrel barely missed Willis as he jumped back. The heavy gun crashed against the counter's surface and Willis staggered further backwards into a shambling tower of boxes. Boxes of Plushes fell around him.

Lance shuffled towards Willis, swinging the rockshocker back and forth in a wide arc. 'I don't have to fire this thing for it to be a weapon. When my son said *go* he meant *go*.'

Arizona remained unmoving. She stood directly in Lance's path. Willis grabbed at her, attempting to wrench her away. Too late, the broad swing of the rockshocker's barrel connected with one side of her head. She swayed, then crumpled to the floor. Lance stood over her, his teeth clenched. Zeb joined him and looked down at Arizona's motionless body.

'Oops,' he said. 'That wasn't meant to happen.'

Willis shoved past Zeb and bent down to her. Dark blood gushed from a wide slice in her head. He touched her cheeks and stroked her blood-soaked hair. He could detect no life in her.

'Why?' he demanded, looking back at them in horror.

'Why indeed?' Zeb said.

Willis rose and glared into Zeb's eyes. They'd changed. They were bottomless pits. And there was something else. *Indeed.* Zeb never said *indeed.* And what was that sound? Like someone yelling from far off – shouted words blown by a gale: *Willis!* And: *Can you hear me?* Willis ran his fingers through his hair, digging his nails into his scalp, trying to press understanding through his cranium and into his muddled brain.

He knew the owner of the distant voice.

Arizona!

Willis glanced down at her. She remained lifeless at his feet.

But there she was again. Clearer. 'Willis!'

A thought struck him. 'She isn't dead at all, is she?' he said. 'Not the real Ari. None of this is real.' He turned to Lance. 'Not you.' He turned to Zeb. 'Not even you.' Willis took a breath. 'Attention, Plush,' he chanced. 'Shut down the game.'

Zeb scoffed. '*Game?* I think you'll find there's no

Plush here to save your butt. You're on your own.'

'Attention, Plush!' Willis hammered out each syllable. 'I said shut—' He broke off, his mouth gaping.

Arizona's hand had appeared. Nothing else, just her hand.

It hovered over her dead form, waving at him. Beckoning him. He reached for it and it pulled away and disappeared. Then it returned and this time stretched towards him. He grasped it and turned to Zeb and Lance. They watched, startled.

Arizona's voice called again and he concentrated on it: 'It's you ... It's not a game ... It's you ... Gameblur!'

Willis understood and squeezed his eyes tight. This is not real, he told himself. None of this is real. He was determined not to open his eyes again until he truly believed those words. And when he did open his eyes, he was just in time to catch the wispy remnants of Zeb and Lance as they dissipated into the air like summer rain steaming off a hot pavement.

Willis no longer stood in a store surrounded by boxes. He stood in a street he didn't recognise. Arizona stared at him, her face wracked with fear. She wrenched her hand from his and held it to herself as if it had been scorched.

Willis shook. His mouth opened and closed. It was dry and hard to speak. 'You're ... alive?'

'Of course I am! I've been following you for hours, steering you away from people and ground traffic. Couldn't you hear me? When you left your room, you were no longer in the game, but you kept acting as if you were.'

'Gameblur,' Willis said, feeling nauseous. He'd been utterly fooled. 'I thought I was in the real world. I thought you'd shut the game down.'

'It was that other thing, pretending to be me. Pretending to shut it down. I could see everything before you left the Plush gamespace of your bedroom and went into gameblur.' She stepped back from him, clutching her hand closer to herself. 'I saw you ... I watched you kissing it.'

Willis's face burnt with humiliation. 'I thought ...' he stammered. 'I ... I'm so sorry. I don't know what to say, how to explain—'

'What's to explain?' she interrupted. 'I was forced to watch every last lovey-dovey moment. I felt like puking.'

Willis blinked at her, the real Arizona who trembled with anger before him. He was still adjusting to all that had happened, trying to work through it in his mind. And now there was this as well. That was all he needed.

Chapter 21

They walked down the street, a small but definite space between them. Willis remembered how they'd held hands last time. And how before leaving the house they'd kissed.

But it had been with a virtual Arizona.

He sighed. 'Look, about what happened ... I'm sorry.'

She didn't look at him. 'I don't want to talk about it.' She kept her face blank, reminding him of the virtual Arizona when they'd found the fake Zeb. He reached for her, suddenly remembered, and pulled his hand away. Too late – she'd seen his instinctive gesture and rubbed her elbow in response, the place where he would have touched her. Anger flared in her eyes.

'When I saw you die like that,' he said, 'it was so shocking.'

She flicked him a look that showed her distaste.

'The virtual you, I mean,' he quickly corrected himself.

'Just tell me where we're going – you did find that out, didn't you?'

Willis remembered how the virtual Arizona had led him to Virtualitee. 'Sort of. The virtual you took care of that. We went into the city, Degraves Street. It wasn't hard to find. At least, it wasn't before. But none of that was real, of course …' His words trailed off. When he looked at her, he saw she was studying him closely.

'You still want to find him, don't you?'

Willis nodded. 'More than ever.'

Arizona dropped her hyperboard to the ground before her. 'Then let's go.'

In one smooth, expert motion, she stepped onto her sleek hyperboard and glided away without looking back. Willis hurriedly leapt onto his. He accidentally kicked it up to top gear and almost bailed off as he sped after her.

They mostly hyperboarded side by side, but at one point where the traffic was thick she sped ahead, performing a varial kickflip – a complex jump and board spin – as she went. Willis watched in awe. She was every bit as adept on the board as her virtual self.

They went to the same location as far as Willis could

recall from his gameblur, but the narrow street wasn't there. They stood for a while, gazing at the forbidding buildings. 'We don't really know if any of it is the same, anyway,' he said in frustration. 'That address might have been part of the gameblur and nothing more.'

Arizona agreed. 'But we've nothing else to go on.'

'I remember these places,' Willis said, pointing at the two stores that had also featured in his gameblur: the divorce bureau and the discount store. *Shop 2* was etched into the glass of the bureau's window. Willis peered at the next premises. It was also empty. *Shop 3* was inscribed above its door. 'But in reality there's no street running between them.'

With no better idea of how to proceed, they spent several hours searching the surrounding area, radiating further and further out in case they randomly stumbled upon the street they were looking for. Willis was amazed at how riddled with laneways and alleys one city centre could be. Finally, at a loss, they returned to the original spot. They pulled up their hyperboards and sat down on the kerb, their boards by their sides.

Willis took care to ensure a gap remained between them. He glanced at Arizona's face and then stared more closely. Tears filled her eyes and though she fought to hold them back they soon spilt down her cheeks.

'Are you okay?' he asked.

She sat up straighter and sniffed back her tears. 'Willis, I want to tell you something.'

'Oh!' Willis couldn't hide his surprise at her sudden frankness.

'When my father lived with us he used to really go at Mum. Both fists. It took a lock and key to keep him away.'

Her words took a moment to sink in. 'He hit you?'

She looked at the ground. 'A couple of times. I could never tell when he came near me if he was gong to hug me or hit me. But Mum really copped it. He – he hurt her pretty badly. And when we were finally rid of him, Mum cracked it bad and needed treatment. I was alone at home for two weeks.'

Willis grimaced but said nothing.

'I remember when she came back, she was crying and saying how much she missed me. She wanted to hug me but at first I thought maybe she would hit me instead, the way Dad used to.' Arizona put her face in her hands, sighed, and then looked back up. 'I ran and hid in my room. I've never let anyone touch me since.'

'How old were you?'

'Ten.'

'No one's touched you since you were ten?' Willis was shocked into silence by her revelation. They sat without speaking for several minutes. He thought about how she'd reached in and held his hand, helping him from his gameblur. Her firm hand had pulled him out of it. He understood now how difficult that must have been for her.

'Not until I pulled you from that gameblur today,' she said.

He let his hand rest near hers and looked at her. 'Thank you.'

'C'mon, let's get out of here,' she said. 'It's getting dark.'

They climbed to their feet. Willis reached for his hyperboard with one foot but suddenly stopped. Unnoticed by them, a crowd of people about their own age had gathered nearby. They stood, ignoring each other, shuffling and looking at the ground, occasionally glancing at the two stores that had featured in Willis's gameblur.

Willis caught Arizona's eye. She shrugged in response. *Your guess is as good as mine.*

He was about to kick his hyperboard into life when he spotted a scrap of paper blowing along the ground. A sudden gust pressed it against the side of the gutter. It was the small figure moving across the paper that grabbed his attention. He stepped from his hyperboard, bent down and picked it up. The words moving at the top of the page read: *Come to Virtualitee and see for yourself.* Beneath the words gyrated a picture of Grimble like the one on the singing card. In response to the warmth of Willis's fingertips on the paper, the tiny Grimble sang out. '*You're virtually there and seeing for yourself,*' it squeaked. '*Ooh indeedy. Yip, yip, yip!*'

Arizona was already moving forward on her hyperboard, but when she saw Willis had stepped from his she stopped awkwardly and almost tumbled off. 'What is it?' she asked, steadying herself.

He gave her the scrap of paper and, as she examined it, he gaped at what unfolded behind her. A thick crack formed in the brickwork between the two stores. Then others. The cracks multiplied rapidly and spread across the wall before merging into one thick, widening fracture. There was a wrenching sound and then, with a groaning yawn, the wall ruptured. Heavy steel girders gave way and exposed shuddering concrete frames, twisted pins protruding from them.

Arizona still gripped the piece of paper. She turned, mouth hanging open. Shattered bricks spat through the dust. Broken cables thrashed and sizzled in the air before they dropped lifeless.

And when at last the dust settled they blinked into a dark wedge of an alley now visible between the two buildings.

CHAPTER 22

Willis and Arizona stepped into the crumbling alleyway. Arizona let the scrap of paper slip from her hands and Willis watched a current of air seize it and whisk it ahead of them. It coiled high, higher even than a pigeon that battled against the gust, until it slapped against a steel parapet on the roof of a building. Willis lowered his gaze and took in the sight: a brightly lit store stood at the end of the alley. A row of wide, gleaming windows on either side of an entrance revealed a games store to end all games stores. Through the windows, Willis could see countless rows of shelves jammed with stock, disappearing into the store's depths.

As they picked their way over the debris, their hyperboards held over their heads, the other kids scrambled ahead of them. One after the other, they slipped through the store's entrance.

'We're not the only ones,' Arizona whispered.

They were the last to arrive at the entrance and paused, looking at it. Willis wanted to turn and leave, but knew he'd never be able to live with himself if he turned tail now. Light globes framed the door and shone in a stroboscopic effect, giving the appearance of an entry into a circus attraction. It was an old-fashioned, heavy wooden door with a brass doorknob and letterbox fixed at its centre. But as Willis reached for the doorknob, the door split in half – right down the centre of the doorknob and letterbox – and smoothly *whooshed* open. '*Virtual greetings,*' it said. '*You've come to Virtualitee to see for yourself.*'

'We certainly have,' Willis said.

They stepped across the threshold and into a giant hypermart, with a maze of towering shelves spreading out before them, all containing virtual games. They dropped their hyperboards in a rack and drifted further in. The ceiling stretched over them as black as the night sky.

'How is it so high in here?' Arizona said. 'The place was one storey from the outside.'

To their far right, before the aisles, stretched a counter, and behind it lurched a tall, dark figure, sorting product. He kept his head bowed as he worked.

They hurried in a different direction, hoping he

hadn't seen them.

'Isn't that the one you called Grimble?' Arizona whispered when they stopped in a long, curving central aisle. 'Does he dress like that all the time?'

'Seems that way.'

'Must be hot under that mask.'

'Mask?' He looked at her in surprise.

'Of course. What else?' She laughed aloud. 'Or perhaps he's totally a hologram. Look how fuzzy he is around the edges.'

Willis disagreed. 'He's not like any hologram I've seen before. And holograms are never fuzzy. No, he's something else again.'

They made their way down one shadowy aisle after another. Figures scuttled up and down. They kept their eyes averted from Willis and Arizona and each other. The shelves were bewilderingly high and stuffed chaotically with games. Gazing up made Willis dizzy; he couldn't do it for long. At their utmost heights, the shelves swayed.

As they turned a sharp bend, they walked directly into a young woman. She jumped at their sudden arrival and her games spilt across the floor. They were all on an ocean theme: scuba diving, snorkelling, deep-sea diving. Willis bent down to help her recover them. She wore thick glasses with round-rimmed frames that accentuated the size of her eyes and the roundness of her face.

'I love the water,' she said. 'I love swimming with fish. But in the real world I'd drown. I can't swim a stroke. So I do it this way. Virtually.'

Arizona rolled her eyes.

The girl straightened and headed off.

'Have fun,' Willis called after her receding back. He turned to Arizona. 'What's your problem?'

Arizona screwed up her lips, smiling stupidly. '*I love swimming with fish.*' She pulled a fish face, complete with bulging eyes.

'Her voice was never that squeaky.'

'Well, you can't say her eyes didn't puff out.'

He pressed his lips together but couldn't help smiling. 'Whose wouldn't with glasses like that?'

They worked their way to the heart of the place. They didn't have a plan; they headed in that direction instinctively.

Arizona pointed. 'Look!' She spoke in an urgent whisper.

Willis followed her gaze and saw Grimble further down the long aisle. He stood motionless, facing away from them. As always, he faded in and out of focus.

Willis backed up along the row and peered once more towards the front of the store. In the distance, Grimble stood bent over the counter. Returning to Arizona, he went up to where the second Grimble stood in the aisle. It was a three-dimensional placard, but in the shadowy aisle it had looked effective.

'It's just a sign,' he called back. 'Zeb and I saw it once at Screamers.'

'It's not even zipanimated,' she said when she got close.

'It's not quite in focus though. That's a clever effect.' A cardboard arm extended from one shoulder. Willis shook it. '*Indeed! Yip, yip, yip.*'

'Stop it,' she said, covering a smirk she couldn't keep from her face. 'That's not what we're here for.'

Willis let his smile drop from his face. 'You're right. But we'll never find Zeb this way.' Willis looked at the placard and knew what he had to do. 'There's only one thing for it.' He could see in her eyes she had guessed what he meant.

'Willis, I'm not sure we should.'

Before she could say anything more, he turned and marched back the way they'd come. He worked around figures hunching over and fingering through the same kind of horrocore Zeb had come to love. One young man turned semi-glazed eyes to Willis then returned to the precious game in his hands. Willis glimpsed its title: *Coffin Boy*. The packaging threw out an image of a coffin with a wooden lid that banged open and shut like a hungry shark. Yep, Willis thought, horrocore.

At the counter, Grimble had a chart spread before him. Willis glanced at it as he walked up. It was a ledger with names in its long columns. Grimble was checking them.

'Excuse me,' Willis said. He spoke without a tremble in his voice, which surprised him.

Grimble looked up with sunglasses as black as death. Willis could discern no glint or reflection in them. He returned to his ledger, running a bony finger down the column of names. Then he raised his head again and faced Willis once more. 'Willis Jaxon?' His smooth grey face did not crease as he spoke. He pointed at the ledger. 'I do not have you listed. At least, not yet.'

'Well, I'm here now, list or no list. And I'm free from that gameblur – was that your doing? That false Virtualitee with its false Zeb nearly fooled me.'

Arizona walked up to stand beside him. 'But it didn't,' she added.

'And who might you be?' Grimble hissed.

'Arizona.'

He looked at her expectantly. She stared back. He sighed. 'Arizona *what*? Full name, please.'

'Arizona Garfunkel.'

'Really? Whatever you say.' He scrutinised his ledger

again. 'You're not here either. I don't have either of you down as even remotely ready. And yet you have both come to the real Virtualitee to see for yourself?'

Willis sucked in his breath, steadying himself. He ignored the stench of Grimble's breath though it stuck to the roof of his mouth like a toxic gas. 'No, we're just looking for our friend. I'll bet his name is on your list. Tell us where Zeb is. We'll collect him and leave.'

'Nothing doing.' Grimble threw up one arm as if to take in the customers browsing the aisles. 'That one boy is worth as much as all my other gamefreaks put together. To have something even more potent than his father was! Ooh, yes indeed. And without the risks of him getting eaten out by Fast. Very nice.'

'His father?' Arizona said. 'What are you going on about? And who or what are you anyway, behind that el cheapo mask?' She reached over and grabbed at his face. Grimble stumbled backwards but wasn't quick enough to avoid her.

'No!' cried Willis. He didn't know why, but it definitely seemed like the wrong thing to do.

Arizona turned to Willis. 'It's just a rubber mask. You know I'd never touch—' The surprise in her eyes said the rest. She turned back to Grimble, her body stiffening. Her hand had embedded in his forehead up to her wrist and her lightly varnished fingernails were clearly visible through the parietal bone at the back of his head.

Willis grabbed her arm and a numbing shock ripped into him. He couldn't let go; he gripped her around the waist with his other arm and tried to haul her away from Grimble. She remained unmoving. The sensation that charged through her and into him was massive. It felt like every dark emotion experienced by humanity had coalesced into a single hard strand of energy. And along that strand hurtled images. Dreamlike, they twisted through his mind. Willis saw myriad long, crisscrossing corridors. Lining the walls of every corridor were terror-stricken faces trapped behind panes of glass. Some faces blistered and peeled, revealing rivers of red over white bone. Others melted, consumed by tendrils of flame. Others still crumbled like dried-up clay, disintegrating to a fine powder that in turn was puffed away by a gasp of wind. Every face Willis saw came to a harrowing end in some way, and it was this terrible parade of fates that was being channelled into the energy that transmitted through Arizona and into him.

Grimble too was rigid, though he'd managed to turn his head in their direction.

Willis became aware of a new sensation. Calm and strong. It seemed to emanate from Arizona. And then she spat words into Grimble's face: 'Get away from me. I do not like physical contact. Least of all yours.' As slight as she was, she thrust herself forwards. Her hand, balled into a fist, now extended from the other side of Grimble's head up to her wrist. She twisted it then yanked backwards, pushing into Willis and wrenching herself free.

Grimble staggered from her, howling. He doubled over and clawed at his face and head.

Arizona slumped against Willis then sank to the floor. Her eyes closed.

Willis bent over her. 'Ari!' He stared at her hand – it was fuzzy. Out of focus. Willis squinted. When he looked again he saw it had returned to normal. After a few seconds, she opened her eyes and peered at him.

'I was wrong,' she whispered. 'It *is* his face.'

Willis looked up at Grimble, leaning over the counter. He held one thin hand to his face. His cheek bubbled and spattered where Arizona's hand had pushed in.

'Your tickets are clipped,' Grimble said. 'Willis Jaxon and Arizona Garfunkel. Your membership's accepted and you're being fast-tracked. Welcome to the final EleMental.' The ledger before him curled up and shrank into a ball the size of a pill. He picked it up and dropped it into his mouth. He belched. 'Yeuck. Underdone. Still, it will do.'

With his free hand, he slammed the counter. The floor shuddered. 'Closing time,' he boomed through the growing tremor. The exit split open in readiness for the departing customers. 'Everybody out. All games will be downloaded direct to your Plush.' He looked at Willis and Arizona. 'Except you two, of course. This is your game now. Play!'

He slammed the counter again and again, and the shuddering grew to a quake. Cracks spread out under their feet and the floor lurched. A bank of nearby shelves rocked back and forth. The first in line lifted and tilted. It crashed into the second, which slammed into the third – on and on. The toppling shelves spread throughout the store. Customers scrambled across the heaving floor, falling and picking themselves up as they hurried through the open door. The young woman Willis had spoken with gestured to them to hurry. She disappeared through the door. Willis heard the door calling after her: *'Thank you for coming to Virtualitee to see for yourself.'*

Grimble continued to slam his fist onto the counter, creating shockwaves.

Arizona dragged herself to her feet. 'I'm not playing in this game, whatever it is. We've got to get out of here.'

'What about Zeb?'

From the corner of his eye, Willis glimpsed a shape run in through the door and disappear down the shaking ruin of an aisle. The sound of wood splintering cut across his thoughts and he turned in time to see a shard of black rock like a giant's pointed finger explode through the floor and block the exit.

'Too late,' Arizona wailed over the din. She sunk to the floor once more. He huddled next to her. But she pointed at something beyond him.

'That rock didn't come up from the ground,' she cried. 'We're—'

He couldn't make out her last words through the noise but he followed her gaze to the windows. The entire store was sinking. The wide windows had already reached ground level. As they scraped against the rubble and rock of the earth, the frames cracked and split, and the glass burst inwards.

Chapter 23

Now quiet. The only sounds Willis heard emanated from the store's walls. They creaked and groaned like an ancient galleon as the store strained from the intensity of the earth that sucked at it, drawing it underground. Willis crouched beneath the counter. Arizona sat across from him. He'd lost sight of Grimble some time ago. Willis guessed he'd moved off.

But now he heard a new sound, something shuffling up from behind him. Willis battled with his fear and did not turn. Then something solid shoved into his back. He slowly twisted around. The thick muzzle of a rockshocker faced him. A mess of limp wires ending in tiny dull globes hung from the end of the muzzle like a clutch of dead baby snakes. Willis stared down the length of the oversized barrel – smothered in symbols

and blood-red words of warning: *Danger! Caution!* –
and into the eyes of Lance Hack.

'Where's that schoffin' son of mine?' Lance said.

Behind Willis, Arizona gasped. 'His son? That's
what Grimble meant. Is it really true?'

Willis shook his head, trying to forget what Ms
Redman had told him. 'He's already got a dad.'

Lance smirked. 'Yeah, right.'

A tremendous shudder knocked Willis backwards
onto Arizona. Lance easily steadied himself without
dropping his weapon. 'Like being back on a spaceball,'
he said.

But Willis saw something Lance couldn't see. A shelf
teetered behind him. Lance looked into Willis's eyes,
clearly registering something was wrong. He turned,
but had time only to hold up one arm in protection.
The tall shelf came crashing down, its highest section
punching Lance flat to the floor.

Willis seized the moment and leapt from beneath
the counter. Arizona jumped up behind him. He
didn't know where to go, but anywhere away from
this madman would do, even if it meant running into
Grimble again.

They had worked their way past a rubble of shelves
when from behind came the sound of a harsh double-
clack. Something warned Willis to stop. Arizona banged

into him. Together they peered back. Lance stood on top of the rubble of shelves, his rockshocker aimed at them. From their position further on, Willis could see that the lowest shelving pinned down a man. The man was conscious and whimpered beneath the weight. The rockshocker in Lance's hands was now lit up, and the once-limp wires fixed to the nozzle's circumference squirmed and thrashed. Sharp pricks of light emitted from each wire head. They flicked over Willis and Arizona, as if gauging their distance and dimensions.

'Well, well, I register a favourable blast area,' Lance said.

'No!' Willis called back.

'Then where's my son?'

'We don't know. We're looking for him too.' Willis decided he might as well tell the truth. 'He's in some kind of trouble with this place. You must know that if you've traced him here. Maybe we could rescue him together?'

'Together?' Arizona whispered beside him.

Willis shrugged. Anything was worth a try.

The disbelief on Lance's face made it clear how he felt about Willis's suggestion. 'Rescue? What d'ya take me for? I wanna teach that boy a lesson he'll never forget.' He tapped something on one side of the rockshocker and the mining tool's snaking lights ceased their flicking and entwined. The combined beam blinded Willis and Arizona.

At that moment, the man beneath Lance's feet groaned. 'Somebody help me,' he called. The rubble shifted slightly as he struggled, setting off a small avalanche that knocked Lance off-balance. Willis and Arizona dropped flat to their stomachs as the rockshocker erupted. A bolt shot past them and embedded itself in the wall beyond. A second blurted into the wall after it.

The wall fractured in two places but otherwise seemed undamaged. Willis and Arizona climbed to their feet and Willis looked around for Lance. Was that the best a rockshocker could do? There he was! Lance had thrown himself flat against a shelf, his arms wrapped about his head. Willis stared at him for long moments, not getting it. Then he peered back at the wall. Where the bolts had embedded, he could make out tiny red lights. Blinking. And the rate of blinking was accelerating. Of course, thought Willis. This was mining equipment – not a weapon. The bolts had to embed in rock first. The real blast was yet to come.

'Down, Ari!' he cried.

He threw himself on her and they fell hard as the explosion walloped over them, punching them against a piece of shelving. They hung onto it as it skittered across the floor and slammed into an aisle with two shelves still standing, rows of games reaching to the ceiling on either side of them. Shaken by the impact, the massive shelves lurched towards each other and toppled. Virtual games rained down upon them, followed by the heavy structures themselves. Willis hunched his back against the onslaught. He knew Arizona lay next to him but could not see her. Pushing himself closer, he waited until the avalanche subsided. When it did, he waited still longer, finding his breath. He was buried in the rubble of games but he could see Arizona's fingers. He reached over and squeezed her hand. She kept her hand in his and squeezed back.

'Listen,' he whispered. 'I hear howling.'

It was like a shrill chorus of frightened children.

They struggled through the rubble until they broke through to the surface. The two shelves above them had slammed into each other and now remained pressed together, forming an arch. The customer Lance had stood over partly protruded from the rubble nearby. The severe angle of his head, pressed to his shoulder, indicated his neck had been broken. Willis winced and looked away.

The source of the howling was easy to find; a ragged hole gaped in the store's wall beyond them, admitting a harsh gale. Through it, Willis could discern only a thick, black emptiness. But the hole was not where Willis's gaze fixed itself: next to the hole, rockshocker slung over his back, stood Lance. His clothes flapped in the wind. Lance returned Willis's gaze, but before he could speak, another voice chimed in.

'Ah, there you are.'

All three turned to see Grimble. It was as if he'd melted into their presence. As he approached Lance, his long overcoat did not so much as rustle in the billowing wind. 'You have been an adept delivery boy.'

Anger flared in Lance's eyes. He swung the rockshocker around and aimed it at Grimble. 'I'm no delivery boy.'

'Of course you are. The best. You have driven to me someone with great potency. Someone who reeks of gameblur – beyond all expectations!'

'You're talking about … my son.'

'And aren't I the lucky one! Like father, like son. And put that thing down, you could hurt someone.' Grimble spoke these last words in the tone of a patient parent. Stepping forwards, he cupped Lance's cheek in one hand and pushed the rockshocker away. Then he looked at Willis and Arizona. 'I've done better than you, Willis Jaxon. You don't even come close to Zeb Redman. He's always been the prize, not you. Plush owner or not. I sent my delivery boy to fetch him. But you and your Plush have helped things along very nicely. Zeb Redman's the purest I've ever come across. I like to think of him as ... my special gameboy. Still, the more the merrier. The more I have, the merrier I'll be, that is. So you're both invited anyway.'

He held out his arms to Lance. 'Come to me. Come and join your son.'

Willis watched, astonished, as Lance lowered the rockshocker and let Grimble's arms fold about him. Grimble raised one hand and his thin fingers stroked Lance's scalp. They appeared to melt together and both shifted in and out of focus until it became difficult for Willis to tell where they joined.

Grimble's face emerged from the shape and turned to Willis and Arizona. 'I like asteroid miners. They may not vent pure gameblur like your friend, but they're still wracked with it. All that Fast-infested gaming. They come ... ready-baked.' He walked over to the edge of the hole, pulling Lance with him. He peered into the hole. Then, with Lance still pressed into him, he jumped through.

Willis and Arizona stared after him for several minutes, as if Grimble might somehow reappear. Finally, they crept towards the hole. Grasping onto the edge, Willis leant forward and through. Rushing air pummelled his face, sucked at his breath and brought tears to his eyes. Across a wide, black expanse, he could make out massive cliffs of granite-like rock. A fissure in the rock that must have been the size of a lagoon for him to see it from this far away stared back like an enormous, unblinking eye. Looking directly down, he saw in the blackness a shape dropping beneath them. The shape circled in the air like a giant bat. It was Grimble with Lance; Grimble held his overcoat across both of them and grasped the rockshocker in one hand.

Willis raised his head and gazed once more across the sweep of emptiness towards the distant wall of rock. He could no longer see the broad fissure cut like an eye. Yes, he could – but it was now much higher. Willis realised what this must mean, as impossible as it seemed. Like Grimble and Lance beneath them, they were falling too.

Swinging back in, he described what he'd seen to Arizona. 'The whole store is in free fall down some massive chasm. That means there's no way we can leave this place. We're trapped.'

She said nothing and he understood her silence – what could she say?

They returned to where the two shelves had jammed together and dug out the mess beneath until they had created a hollow. Willis found the placard of Grimble that he'd joked with. They crawled inside the hollow and pulled the placard over the top to close it off. He knew they were alone in the descending shop, but it deadened the howling wind – and it felt safer.

After a while, Willis spoke. 'That bubbling on Grimble's face? That happened when Zeb touched him too, the first time we met him.' He shook his head as a new thought occurred to him. 'You know, you and Grimble – you both hate touching.'

'But my skin doesn't exactly snap, crackle and pop, thank you very much. And he'd no problems touching that man before. Lance.'

'True. It's as if he can't handle being touched unless you're like him. Wracked with gameblur. And you haven't touched anyone for so long, maybe your touch somehow packs a punch.'

She moved closer to him. 'Well, I'm catching up on my touch quota now, anyway.'

'I'll say.'

They huddled together, trying to forget their predicament. Neither slept, but Willis did achieve a certain groggy state that helped time slip by. The howling of the wind through the hole became a background noise he could almost ignore.

After a time Arizona shook him. He sat up, alert. 'Listen,' she said. 'There's a new noise. It's scaring me.'

He could hear it too. A sharper sound mixed in with the howling. 'Squeaking? Like mice?'

'You think I'm worried about mice? It's something else.'

He concentrated on the sound. And then it came to him. Screaming. And with every moment it grew more distinct until it was shrill and piercing. The abyss down which the store plummeted, Willis guessed, acted as an echo chamber funnelling the sound up to them. That could only be by design, a greeting to newcomers. As the sound grew, it separated into distinct, painful strands of sound like many tiny buzzing wasps puncturing his eardrums, boring into his brain and planting minute eggs of torture there.

He clapped his hands over his ears. Through it all, he recognised one scream. He seized Arizona.

'I know this has to be some Grimble trick,' he yelled. 'But I recognise one of those screams. Zeb's down there!'

'Are you ready to game
or not?'

Grimble, 2050

LEVEL 4:
HERE
COMES
THE FLOOD

CHAPTER 24

Willis and Arizona hugged each other, certain the free-falling store must be rushing towards the base of the chasm they plunged down. How else did the screams they could hear reach them? Teeth clenched, bodies clamped together, legs shoved against their surroundings for support, they braced for the impact and their likely obliteration.

But when the moment came, the store slowed and they landed on the chasm floor with no more than a soft thud that sent a shudder through the rubble of games beneath them.

They dragged themselves from their makeshift hollow, picked their way over the rubble, and stepped out through the hole. They found themselves on a wide, newly made street. Willis could smell the fresh tar. He stared around in disbelief. They stood at the bottom of an abyss, a deep rent in the earth. And yet they were on a street?

It was the sort of street Willis would have expected to find in an industrial part of town – no residences, but plenty of warehouses. The wreckage of the Virtualitee store sat on a stretch of bare ground beyond the kerb and before one of the warehouses. Willis looked more carefully and realised there were only two warehouses, one on either side of the street. But they stretched into the never-ending darkness in both directions. He looked up. The void down which they'd descended hung over them like a starless, moonless night sky.

But there were no screams. Whatever trick it was that had allowed them to be heard was now gone. Though it was dark, a dull light permeated the air; strong enough to see around, though fragmented. It cast no shadows. Willis searched around but couldn't fathom its source.

He turned to see Arizona staring at him. 'Any ideas?' she whispered.

He could hear her fear and he felt it too. He took her hands. 'Ari, we're stuck some place deep beneath the earth without a clue how to find Zeb. But do you know what? One part of me actually feels good. For once, I'm not just following. My parents. Zeb. Anybody. I'm doing things for myself.'

'Okay. Sounds nice. So what do we do?'

He paused. 'I've no idea.'

Then they heard it: the dull roar of a massive engine. They ran back and hid behind the store. The ground rumbled beneath them. And the louder the roar became, the greater Willis's confusion grew. He could discern no shape emerging from the darkness in either direction. Until ...

A few metres in front of them, the street's surface exploded.

A mass of rotating blades and clacking mechanical claws mushroomed from the ground, followed by a long, revolving body the size of a small apartment block. Hard green lasers needled out, emanating from the hub of each spinning blade. The lasers lacerated the ground and cut up the air, spiking out endlessly. They were like no laser beams Willis had witnessed before, fiercer than anything a hyperboard's erupter could generate. As the colossal mole-machine cranked along the street, the air bristled with its sounds: the howl of the engine, the spit and zing of the lasers, the grating of inner gears, the whine of blades.

Then, like a glitch in an old game, it froze.

A deafening silence filled the darkness.

'What's happening?' In the new silence, Arizona's whisper was a shout.

They waited several minutes. When nothing changed, they came out of hiding and tentatively approached the gigantic vehicle. Dirt hung in the air on all sides, caught mid-spray from the blades. Static laser-shots spiked high into the chasm over them, disappearing into the darkness that led to the earth's surface many kilometres above.

Arizona walked to the other side of the vehicle. Suddenly she gasped and pointed into the air over it. 'Look.'

Willis followed her line of sight but could only see grains of dirt suspended in space. She beckoned to him. He came and stood beside her and saw it too.

From this perspective, the shades and patterns of airborne, motionless dirt took on a specific shape. They formed words.

Fourth EleMental: Earthcore

Willis looked at everything with new insight. He indicated the motionless machine. 'It's a boss enemy,' he said at last. 'I think Grimble has us back in *EleMental*. He's determined to keep us gameplaying. It's like he's a Plush all to himself.' He drew in a deep breath and called out. 'Attention, Grimble. What's going on? Are we in a game?'

'Ah! Just waiting to see how long it would take you two to figure things out.' It was Grimble's voice. 'Welcome to Virtualitee. You're here, seeing things for yourself. And now I must get you up and gaming – can't have the two of you wandering about the place and getting up to no good. The gameplay's the thing, as they say. What weapons do you choose?'

'Is this place all just one big game?'

'Virtualitee? A game? I suppose it is. Maybe. If I say it is.'

'Where's Zeb?' Arizona yelled.

'Still on about Zeb? Now, there's someone who doesn't bother needling me with silly questions about whether this is all a game or not. He just games! Games, games, games, games, games. What a special gameboy he is. So enough questions. What weapons do you choose?'

Willis sighed. He glanced at the monstrous contraption that loomed before them. 'How about a jet fighter?'

'On your energy points? Not likely.'

'A zap tank?'

'Nope.'

'Grenades?'

'Nope.'

Willis thought for a moment. 'Just out of interest, what *are* our energy points?'

'Wait a minute.' There was a moment's silence. 'Still

checking.' Another moment of silence. 'Ah yes, you're both on zero.'

Willis groaned. 'Zero? Okay. So what weapons do we qualify for?'

'Checking again. Ah yes, lots! Dagger, catapult, peashooter, strong handgrip, belittling curses—'

'Stop,' Willis interrupted. 'How about non-weapons? What's available there?'

'Let me see. Ah yes, increased running and jumping ability, improved eyesight—'

'Hold it a moment!' Willis turned to Arizona. 'Ari, any idea where our hyperboards are?'

'Lost somewhere in the store.'

'Can I choose a hyperboard?' Willis called out.

'*Hyperboard?*' whispered Arizona. Willis stilled her with a hand signal.

'*Hyperboard?*' said Grimble's voice. 'Why not. It could be interesting to see how you plan to use it. Granted.'

A bright red hyperboard coasted out of the gloom. Its erupter was off. It was as if it had been pushed from a short distance away. Willis stopped it with his feet.

'I choose a hyperboard too,' said Arizona.

'The female companion also chooses a hyperboard,' said Grimble's voice.

Correction, thought Willis, not a female companion – a champion hyperboarder.

'Well, let's see if we have a hyperboard in a nice colour for the female companion,' said the Grimble game voice. 'Ah!'

Another hyperboard appeared. It was also red but with a decoration of daisies linked in a chain about its edges.

'It'll do,' she said.

Willis tried to hide his amusement.

'Stop with that face,' Arizona growled. 'All right, I've followed your lead, now what?'

'Are you ready to game or not?' Grimble interrupted.

'Hang on a second,' Willis called back. 'This hyperboard needs adjusting.' He pretended to fiddle with the erupter on his hyperboard and spoke in a lower tone to Arizona. 'As a gamer I'd suggest jumping on our hyperboards, kicking them back, and putting some distance between us and this ugly thing. At least until we figure out how to earn enough points to do it some serious damage.'

'Good plan.' Arizona jumped on her hyperboard, one leg stuck out ready for a kick-start.

'So ...' Willis whispered.

Arizona turned and looked at him.

'—that's exactly what we're not going to do,' Willis finished.

'Ah.' Arizona stepped off the hyperboard.

Willis motioned her over to him and spoke into her ear. 'There's no way we should gameplay. That's what he wants – so that's exactly what we shouldn't do. Didn't you just hear him say he doesn't want us wandering about, up to no good?'

She nodded.

'Then that's what we should be doing!'

He picked up his hyperboard and tucked it under his arm. 'C'mon, we'd better get moving before Grimble starts carrying on about gaming again.'

'Where?'

'Attention, Grimble,' Willis called out. 'Resume game.' He pointed to the warehouse closest to them. 'There.' He broke into a run towards it, Arizona close at his heels.

The mole-machine's sounds echoed around them once more, and the dirt previously suspended in space sprayed through the air. Willis glanced back and saw the machine rise up on an axis of wheels and swing in their direction. As they ran, they ducked under and leapt over laser shots that swept at them from the machine.

Slamming against the warehouse wall, Willis spied a door about thirty metres to his left. Its features were only visible when pressed flat to the wall. They hunkered down, staying close to the wall, and bolted for it.

The door was vault-like in size yet merely sported a rusty, old-fashioned padlock. Willis smashed the lock with the blunt end of his hyperboard.

'Not a weapon, eh?' said Arizona with a look of admiration.

They heaved the door open.

Chapter 25

Across the long threshold of the warehouse's heavy door lay bedlam. The screams had returned. Willis and Arizona stepped into a corridor and tried to pick out one scream in particular from the many.

Giving in, they wandered a maze of corridors. Fixed into the walls on either side of every corridor were wide gamespace windows. Glowing control panels of dials, slide controls, switches and displays were set beneath them. Willis and Arizona ran to window after window, in awe of the diverse worlds within. People struggled in all manner of game scenarios: sinking ships; seething snake pits; burning starships; collapsing buildings; crocodile-infested waters; battledroid warfields ...

'And I bet they're all Plush owners!' Willis had to shout to be heard above the racket.

A panel display beneath each window named a

location: *Charlottesville, USA*; *Luton, UK*; *Melbourne, Australia*. Next to each location was a date – the date when the gamer took out Virtualitee membership, Willis guessed.

'Plushes the world over are jacking into Virtualitee,' Willis called.

'And on the spacefronts,' Arizona called back.

He nodded. 'It's like we're wandering around the guts of a massively-multiplayer online game. And none of them have a clue.'

There were other displays with calculations. *Levels and Missions Racked Up. Wins and Losses. Life Expectancy.* Some made less sense: *Attitude. Values. Beliefs. Self-esteem. Resilience.*

Arizona stared from the controls to Willis. 'How can beliefs and attitudes be calculated?'

Willis shrugged and pointed to another display beneath all of them. *Cumulative Value.*

'It all gets added up?' She shook her head.

'Check this out,' Willis said. 'These slide controls are for intensity.'

They stood at a window with an ocean-diving game scenario. A young woman fought a school of great white sharks. Willis indicated a row of controls set apart from the others: *Smell, Taste, Touch, Hunger, Hostility* and *Frenzy.* 'I think they're for the sharks. I wonder what would happen if ...' The control panel gleamed as he slid them all up.

As they watched, the sharks attacked with greater vigour, sweeping close to the sandy bottom. The woman easily speared them.

'It's her. From the store. Do you remember?'

'I do. She's good.' Arizona peered closely. 'She's doing more than *swimming* with fish though.'

One speared shark reared belly up and jerked in convulsions. They watched as its mouth yawned wide and it retched. Long, bone-white creatures floated from the gaping orifice. Some drifted out from the gut of the shark on their sides, as if stunned by birth. But they quickly righted themselves and looked around. They were fat, ugly eels with slitted mouths that split open to reveal rows of needle-sharp teeth.

'What's this game?'

Willis looked. 'Eelements. I know it, Ari. Not this scenario. But it's the Third EleMental level – the one with the bogus you.'

Still convulsing, the shark bloated and ruptured, its grey-blue and white sheen bursting into lumps of pink meat that sent the other sharks into a feeding frenzy, and from deep within its round carcass emerged a compacted bundle that began unravelling into a writhing mass – more of the long white eels.

They broke apart and joined the others, becoming a tightly knit school that moved towards the woman like an underwater cloud.

The woman's eyes widened behind her goggles. A mass of bubbles burst from her mouth. And, though he could not hear her, Willis knew what she shouted: *Weapons!* But the game wasn't providing anything beyond what she already had. She sent a spear at the school. It was a neat shot and took out at least three. But that was all she had time for. The school with its thousands of needle-teeth sped towards her. She opened her mouth as if to cry out, and began swallowing water and choking.

'Turn it down!' Arizona yelled. They sprang at the controls and yanked them back. The approach of the menacing fish instantly slowed. Still choking, the woman turned and swam away.

'I don't get it. She seemed in true danger. Her face! It was so full of fear.'

They wandered for a long time, uncertain what else to do. The screams and hollering continued, emanating from the countless rooms. It created a continuous sound, a hell saturating the air.

'I remember him too,' said Willis, gazing through another window. A young man lay on his back in a mahogany coffin. The viewing window displayed the nightmarish gameplay as a clear dissection through layers of earth and polished wood, though Willis knew the gamer would not have been able to see it that way. The man lay on his back, gagging for air, punching and kicking in his cushioned surroundings. It was as if he had woken from a deep sleep to a terrible misunderstanding. He began clawing at the underside of the lid with bleeding fingers. If he broke through by some miracle, he still had six feet of rock and dirt to contend with.

Arizona shivered. 'What kind of games are these?'

They dragged the controls down, and when they looked up, they saw the gamer successfully force the lid open and squirm his way through the compact earth, pushing rocks aside. He broke through to daylight, relief spreading across his face, and lay on the ground, sucking in air.

'C'mon,' Willis said. 'We've got to keep searching.'

They wandered down winding corridors without talking, glancing through windows. After a while, Willis found it easier not to examine game scenarios. It was too distressing. He became adept at zooming in on the gameplayer's face and quickly moving on.

✳ ✳ ✳

They finally turned into a corridor different to all the others. In the distance, they could see it came to an end.

And a scream reached them that Willis recognised.

'I have you now!' Zeb's voice bawled.

Chapter 26

For once, the corridor did not bend into yet another or, worse still, split into two or three new ones. When Willis and Arizona reached the dead end, two gamespace windows lay on either side of them. It was as if these were the final two windows. And there was something else new: alongside each window stood a door. One of the gamespace windows lay in darkness, suggesting no gameplay, but the other window was alive with flashing, spiralling colours. A battle raged inside. At the centre of things, on a grassy hillock, stood Zeb. He was clad in metallic battle armour and wielded a small rocket launcher in both hands as creatures of all shapes came at him. The creatures – skeletons, zombies, trolls, battledroids, wolves, all with ridiculous smiley faces – seemed to be built of coloured blocks. As Zeb fired at them, they exploded, only to reassemble an instant later. Zeb blasted them repeatedly. They gave him little time to pause.

'What kind of game is this?' Willis cried. 'He's just endlessly button mashing in an endless game.'

'No,' Arizona said. 'We're not looking into a Plush game played somewhere else, like all those others. He's right here. And in full-blown gameblur. Can't you see?'

Willis stared at the scene, concentrating. After a moment, he caught a flicker in the air. He concentrated harder and caught a glimpse of a bare room. Zeb leapt about recklessly at its centre, dressed in rags and lashing out at emptiness. Then the blinding colours of battle returned.

'He's like Grimble now,' Willis said. 'Consumed by gameblur.'

For an instant, Zeb turned to where Willis and Arizona stood gazing in. Willis's heart thumped but Zeb turned away again. The gameblur continued to flicker now and then as Willis watched, giving him further glimpses of Zeb leaping about in a blank room.

'Zeb!' Willis shouted. Arizona shouted too. But, though close, he remained deaf to their calls.

Arizona seized Willis's arm. 'He doesn't even know we're here!'

'Let's tell him.'

Clutching his hyperboard, Willis opened the door and strode into the room. He found himself immediately immersed in Zeb's gameblur. This close, the grassy landscape was a hard, glossy plastic. The whole environment was bewildering, with myriad brightly coloured blocks and hard angles. The only curved lines belonged to Zeb's moving form.

A weight suddenly pushed down on Willis's shoulders and wrapped about him. He jerked his arms in alarm, discovering he was now suited up like Zeb. Gameblur was strong down here!

Zeb swung around to face him. 'Willis? How'd *you* get here? This game's not multiplayer.'

Close up, Zeb's dull eyes and his worn, sallow face shook Willis.

'Zeb, we're here to help.'

Zeb seemed taken aback. But at that moment, a row of coloured blocks grew out of the ground and Zeb turned. The blocks formed into a grinning soldier brandishing an oversized machine-gun. It was hard to take it seriously, given the many coloured blocks that formed it and its silly grin. It growled and snarled and growled again, as if it read Willis's thoughts and was eager to communicate its deadliness – that its only call of duty was their immediate demise.

Zeb took it out with a blast from his weapon, shattering it into tiny blocks. 'Just shoot,' he said. 'You can always work on looking evil later.'

Arizona appeared in the room and ran to Willis's side. She too was suited up in the same metallic battle gear.

'Arizona? You're here too?' He held up one hand to indicate they should listen. 'Score!' he cried out.

'Zeb Redman: two hundred and fifty points,' said Grimble's voice in the air. 'Blocko Fiends: zero.'

'Blocko Fiends?' Arizona spoke with incredulity.

'Hear that?' Zeb said. 'I'm winning. But you'd better go. You're not in this game and I can't afford to lose any points.'

'Why can't you?' Willis asked. 'Zeb, do you have any idea where you are?'

'Of course. I'm working through this first-person shooter,' he said. 'I got it from Virtualitee when I went to see for myself.'

'Zeb, you haven't even left Virtualitee. And you're terminally stuck in your own gameblur.'

'Huh?'

'Just tell me one thing: are you having fun?'

'I'll say.' But his smile looked half-hearted. 'Though I'm pretty worn out, to tell you the truth.'

Arizona cut in. 'Do you think you're in Willis's bedroom? On his Plush?'

Zeb peered around him in obvious confusion. 'I …
uh …'

'How long have you been gaming for?' Willis asked.
'Do you even know?' That hit home. Willis could see it
in Zeb's dull eyes.

''Course I know,' Zeb said defensively.

'Then answer. How long?'

'Well, I've been waiting for a save point for …
for …'

'Yeah?'

'I can't remember.'

'Because there isn't one.' Willis threw his arms wide,
gesturing around him. 'This isn't normal, Zeb. You've
gotta see that.'

Zeb suddenly pointed over the back of their heads.
'Duck!' he bellowed. Willis and Arizona dropped to
the ground as a bulky, grinning dragon – entirely
constructed from coloured blocks – bore down on them,
hard plastic claws outstretched. Zeb stood his ground
and pumped rocket after rocket into it. The beast
screeched and burst into wild flames.

'Guys,' Zeb said, 'you'd better go. You're totally
wrecking my gameplay here.'

'Score,' said Grimble's voice, as if on cue. 'Zeb
Redman: two hundred and fifty points; Blocko Fiends:
zero.'

Zeb relaxed and smiled. 'Hear that? The game's telling me the score before I've even asked for it. And I'm winning.'

'*Two hundred and fifty points?*' Willis felt exasperated. 'That's what you were before. You're having the same score shoved at you the whole time.' He grabbed Zeb's arm. 'C'mon, we've got to get you away from here.'

Zeb tried to pull away but Willis kept his grip firm. It didn't require much effort. Zeb was weak. Now that Willis touched him, he could feel him tremble under his grasp.

There was a solid thud – the sound of a door thumping shut – and they turned in its direction. A door – a plain door, one not made from blocks – sat in a small meadow beyond them. Hinged to emptiness. As they watched, Lance marched through it. He wore the thick moon-grey jacket, pants and bulky antigrav boots that Willis had first seen him in. The heavy rockshocker hung across his back. 'What's going on here, son?' he cried.

'I—' Zeb began, then stopped, confused.

Behind Lance, the door dissolved into the air. Willis glanced around, seeing no gameplay about them. Everything had dropped off for a moment, as if Zeb's gameblur had been temporarily distracted, or somehow commanded to take a brief respite.

Lance sneered at Willis and Arizona. 'Why aren't you two outside battling the mighty earthcorer? I put a lot of effort into coming up with that.'

'You?' Arizona asked. 'How do you know about it?'

Willis pointed directly at Lance. 'I'll tell you how he knows. He's Grimble.'

Lance clapped his hands together and broke up in laughter. 'I'm *who*?'

'You heard me. What have you done with the real Lance?'

'Er, I don't think he is, Wil,' Arizona interjected.

Lance fiddled in his pockets. 'I know I have them here somewhere. Ah!' He pulled out a pair of ordinary black sunglasses, held them out for the others to see, then put them on. 'And now?' he said. 'Do I look like Grimble, now?'

They glanced at each other and back at Lance. He looked idiotic in the cheap sunnies. They shook their heads.

'Perhaps I was wrong,' Willis said.

Lance's face changed behind the glasses. The frames grew thicker and the lenses grew darker until they reflected nothing. And Willis could see the remnants of the sore left by Arizona's touch, fading, but still discernible on his cheek. His clothes also changed, shifting from the dirty miner's clothes to the familiar black garb of Grimble Dower. Only the rockshocker remained hanging from his back. 'Did I trick yer?' he said, imitating Lance's voice. 'Now answer my question, why are you here and not gaming? You've got to be in it to win it, gamefreak.'

'We're not in any game you wanted us in,' Willis said. 'And I reckon that gives us a better chance of winning.'

'Indeed? It's not how you play the game, it's how I win and you lose. And let's see who's winning right now, shall we? Attention, *me*. Score!'

'Score,' rumbled Grimble's game voice around them. 'Grimble Dower: three hundred points; Zeb Redman and his ring-in gamemates: two hundred points and falling. Losing, losing, losing.' Grimble's mouth never moved during the game-voice announcement.

'Nice trick,' said Willis.

'And that wasn't two hundred and fifty points this time,' said Arizona.

Willis spoke rapidly in her ear. 'The score's the one thing that's been keeping Zeb here.' He turned to his old gamemate. 'Zeb, come with us. You're not even winning now.'

'The score!' Zeb said. 'I've got to get back to my gameplay.'

'Score,' said Grimble, aloud this time. 'Zeb Redman: one hundred points. And falling. A plummet from the summit, you might say.'

'Well,' said Arizona, 'finally he's saying the scores in person.'

Zeb turned and looked at Grimble. 'He's giving the scores? And I'm losing?'

'Winning, losing, it doesn't matter – you're stuck in gameblur. Grimble's got ideal conditions set up here. You should see it; Plush gamers are jacked in like rows and rows of battery hens.'

Grimble hissed.

Zeb gripped his head. 'My mind feels so fogged up. I—'

'Control it, Zeb. This is real life we're talking about here. Not gaming.'

'He says he's my father.'

Grimble pulled off his sunglasses. Behind them, once more, was the leering face of Lance. 'Course I am.'

Arizona gripped one of Zeb's hands and looked into his eyes. 'Lance might not be your father.'

Willis grabbed Zeb too and shook him. 'And this guy's not Lance, so he's not even in the running.'

Arizona added, 'And he's so riddled with gameblur that when he gets a touch of reality' – without warning, she lunged forwards – 'it hurts.' She caught Grimble on the arm. All three of them remained connected. And now Grimble. Her hand pushed into his elbow and poked through to the other side. Willis felt the cold bolt rush from her and through him.

Lance's features melted back into Grimble's. He lurched away, falling to his knees. The pain seemed to strike through him like an electric charge.

Arizona fell too, dropping her hyperboard. She dragged Willis and Zeb with her into a heap on the ground. But this time she recovered quickly. Struggling to her knees, she called out, 'Quick, Zeb, while we've got a chance!'

'You've got to win back control over your gameblur and shut it down,' Willis urged him.

They helped Zeb struggle to his feet. 'How?' Zeb asked.

'Knowing that it comes from inside you has to be a start. Then control it. Don't let it control you.'

Zeb bent over, his eyes pressed tight. Their surroundings wobbled and Willis glimpsed the bare room beneath everything. He saw, too, the second door, the one Grimble had entered from as Lance. Then the image blinked away and they stood once more in the clear, solid images of Zeb's gameblur. Zeb slumped to the ground and smiled feebly. 'It's too hard, guys. Get away. I can let the gameblur wash back over me. After a while I'll forget you were ever here.'

Willis grimaced at the words, feeling defeat rise in him. Yet Grimble was still on his knees – Arizona had given him quite a shock. They still had a chance. Willis glanced at her; tears smeared her face. He saw Zeb peer at her too.

'Don't, Ari,' Zeb mumbled. 'I'm not worth it. I still haven't forgiven myself for taking your money.' He looked at Willis. 'I've messed you both round.' He closed his eyes and dropped his chin to his chest.

'Zeb!' they both cried.

Zeb opened his eyes – just a bleary slit. 'Wil Boy?' he mumbled. 'I can't win anymore. I'm ... a loser.'

'Oh no you're not. You're a winner. You've always been a winner. Concentrate.'

Zeb stared into Willis's face. Willis could see him trying, garnering what strength he had. Willis gripped Zeb shoulders, as if trying to push his own strength into his friend's body.

'The gameblur's breaking up,' Arizona said.

Willis could see in Zeb's face that he saw it too. Zeb tried to stand but stumbled backwards. They grabbed him, one on each side, and helped him to his feet. He remained hunched over slightly, still working hard within himself. Shreds of the plain room appeared in place of the gameblur. It was not like the folding at the end of a game. There was no tornado. No spinning pinpoint of light. Instead, their surroundings fell away like scraps of bark flaking from a dead silver gum. When at last they stood in an empty room, Zeb stared around and then down at his ragged clothing. He shook his head in disbelief.

'Welcome back to reality, Zeb,' Willis said. 'Or what passes for it in this place at least.'

'Grimble's Virtualitee,' said Arizona.

'Indeed, *my* Virtualitee,' said a voice. 'Let me see, how does this thing work?'

The three of them turned in the direction of the voice. Grimble, now recovered, stood near them grappling with the rockshocker. His thin fingers fiddled with a bolt at the back – the trigger mechanism.

Chapter 27

They didn't wait for Grimble to figure out how to operate the rockshocker. Willis and Arizona snatched up their hyperboards, then each grabbed one of Zeb's arms and yanked him towards the door through which Grimble had earlier entered.

Though it was dark, Willis knew immediately where they now stood. It was the wide side strip where he and Arizona had been before, outside the warehouse. Everything seemed the same except for the appearance of a large industrial waste container standing off to one side.

Willis groaned and pointed to the middle of the street: the mole-machine – or earthcorer, as Grimble had called it – stood silent in the shadows. He sensed it knew they were there. Was watching them. Perhaps waiting for them to make the first move.

'What's that?' Zeb whispered.

'Let's just say you do *not* want to see it in action. Not even you, Zeb.'

Without discussion they about-faced and collectively gasped. The door was gone.

Zeb turned and slumped to the ground with his back to the warehouse wall. 'I've had it,' he mumbled. 'You've gotta think of something, Wil Boy.'

Arizona crouched next to Zeb and looked up at Willis. 'Can't we just yell *shut down* or something?'

'I wish,' said Willis. 'But down here there's no Plush to give commands to. We're in Grimble's gamespace now, not a game controlled by someone's console.'

She put her head in her hands. 'It's like a nightmare you can't wake up from.'

Willis kept his back to the wall but turned away from them. Their reliance on him felt overwhelming. But if there was anything the small amount of gaming he'd experienced had taught him it was this: if you let your losses get to you, you'd never win. Ever. Good gamers knew they would win in the end. So long as you hung in there and kept trying, you couldn't fail. Learn from your mistakes. Get better as you go. Ditch tactics that don't work. Try new ones.

There was no doubt in Willis's mind that Zeb was an incredible gamer. He appeared to have a natural talent. But down here in Virtualitee, that counted for nothing. His special Zeb magic seemed all used up. Willis remembered how – all that time ago – Zeb had left him far behind in the Hall of the Mountain Dragon. While Zeb scored brilliantly somewhere in the depths of the game, Willis clumsily scaled the cliff face, hampered by a rock, his wizzpick set on slow. Yet if there was one thing Willis was better at than Zeb, it was losing. From losing you learned about getting up and trying again. It took him a long while but he climbed that cliff face and he struggled into the mouth of that cave. And, given time, Willis knew he would have finally battled the crown off that Mountain Dragon. Perhaps he even would have hacked the creature's head off, as Zeb had done. Willis wasn't a natural winner like Zeb. But he was certain of this: giving up was *not* the thing to do.

Yet how did you escape someone when you were caught in a world entirely of their devising? Because that's what Virtualitee was – Grimble's manufactured world. Moulded from his gamespace. Willis pursued the idea further and suddenly understood something. Grimble needed gameblur to create his vast gamespace. He and gameblur were so inextricably entwined, without it he could not survive. And the Plush console was his way to generate and suck the gameblur from others. The multiplayer gaming in all the corridors had to be a rich source of gameblur for him, as were all the hard-gaming miners, Lance being the pick of them, even if they were riddled with Fast. And Zeb? Zeb was the big prize. Grimble believed he was Lance's son. He was obviously hoping for a Lance replacement. New and improved – younger and Fast-free.

Willis turned back to Arizona and Zeb. 'To escape Grimble, we have to reduce his source of gameblur if we can.'

Arizona quickly grasped his point. 'Taking Zeb away from Grimble should have weakened him.'

'Which is why he wants him back so badly,' Willis said. 'So if we keep Zeb from him, maybe he'll get weaker. And maybe we can find a way out of here.'

'That's a lot of maybes, but anything's worth a try.'

'Zeb,' Willis asked, looking at him, 'in a normal game, if you're losing this badly, what would you do?'

Zeb answered slowly. 'I've never lost before. I guess I might look for a cheat. Game writers sometimes stick them in to move around more easily.'

'Only one problem,' Arizona said. 'This is the furthest thing from a normal game. No easy way out for us. In this place, there could be games within games, for all we know. We could be dashing into one after another.'

'You're right!' Willis exclaimed.

She jumped in response to his sudden reaction. 'I am? About what?'

'Grimble might have used that new door to get around easily, like a cheat, but there are no easy cheats for us.' He indicated the mole-machine. 'He's landed us back in this same game again, but games happen anywhere. We don't have to be outside. What's the bet we haven't even left the room where we found Zeb?' He stepped from the wall. 'You know, this might give us a new strategy. A good gameplayer continually thinks up new strategies and then tries them out. Ain't that right, Zeb?'

Arizona and Zeb struggled to their feet. They looked perplexed.

'What new strategy?' Zeb asked.

'This.' Willis gazed around and took a few more steps from the wall. 'Where are you, Grimble?' he called.

The mole-machine roared into life, its laser shots puncturing the air as it whirled into action. It lumbered towards them.

'Oh no,' said Arizona. 'You've set it off.'

'And what's the bet Grimble's at the dials!' Willis said. He thought it through. Where would the gamespace window be? It came to him immediately. He jabbed a finger at the waste container in front of them. 'I just know he'd want a front-row seat.'

Arizona squealed and pointed.

A searing rod of laser light swept at them from the machine. They leapt over it. Another came an instant later, blistering through the air from the opposite direction. This time they pressed themselves to the ground and then leapt back to their feet.

'He's really tweaking those dials,' Arizona said.

'And we're going,' added Willis. He kicked the back end of his hyperboard and caught it as it sprang up. He elbowed its small erupter and it kicked into a start. The sudden thrust almost pulled it from his grasp. Hanging on, he swung it around and hurled it at the waste bin. It hit with a crack and bounced off. The bin trembled and blinked out of existence, but immediately reasserted itself. Yet in the instant it had been gone they'd caught a glimpse of Grimble standing behind a gamespace window, at the panels.

'Ha!' shouted Willis in vindication. 'But how do we get through?'

'Get down!' Arizona shouted.

Willis turned in time to see her spinning her hyperboard the same way he'd done. She manoeuvred like an Olympic discus champion. Her aim was a little lower than his had been and he realised she was aiming straight at Grimble. Zeb and Willis dropped to the ground.

This time, as the hyperboard hit the container bin its surface stretched. The speeding hyperboard dragged it inwards until the container bin transformed into the image of the gamespace window and shattered, knocking Grimble to the floor. Instantly the ground wrenched beneath their feet like a giant tablecloth. All of their surroundings followed, including the mole-machine. Everything was dragged into a spinning, tight tornado that shrank into a pinpoint of light and disappeared with a *pop*.

And there now was Grimble. He lay on the floor in the corridor beyond the shattered gamespace window.

'Not sure if that was what I meant by a cheat,' Zeb said. 'But it sure was effective.'

'And that's not the way your gameblur ceases,' Willis said, rising from the floor. 'No breaking up or falling away in shreds. That was how regular gamespace folds up. He doesn't have your powerful gameblur to draw from, so he's resorted to using more conventional gamespace to try and trap us. He has to be getting weaker.' He looked around. He'd been right. They were in the room where they'd originally found Zeb. He snatched up his hyperboard. 'C'mon. Before Grimble tries something else.'

Supporting Zeb as best they could, they hurried through the original door and into the corridor. Grimble was still sprawled on the floor before the shattered gamespace window. They stood at the dead end of the corridor and he lay between them and the maze of corridors beyond. With no other option, they hurried across to the opposite room. The door opened with no trouble.

CHAPTER 28

When Willis slammed the door behind him, grey shadows enveloped them. He turned and wedged the lip of his hyperboard under the door. Then he, Arizona and Zeb stood in the silent room and waited.

When nothing happened, Arizona whispered, 'Why do you suppose he's not trying to follow us? He must have recovered by now.'

'Maybe because he knows there's no way out of here,' Zeb said.

Willis didn't say anything but inside he had the same fear. And not just about the room. About the whole place.

They stood silent for a few more seconds.

'Where do you suppose we are?' Arizona said. 'It's too dark to see.'

Gradually Willis could make out shapes. To his

astonishment, the surroundings looked vaguely familiar. As he stared, he distinguished the dim outline of a sofa. And something hovered over it, as if suspended in the air. An oval shape, like a clouded moon. The murky shape gradually became more distinct until he saw it didn't hang in the air at all. It was attached to a body, which sat on the couch. The oval shape was a face. And it gazed at him without expression. He recognised the face and pushed back a desire to turn and run from the room. He steeled himself and stepped closer to be sure.

'Um, Zeb,' he said. 'We've found Lance. The real one.'

The others joined him. The man stared sightlessly through them.

'Do you recognise where he is?' Zeb said.

'Is it your living room?' Willis asked. His eyes had now adjusted enough to see a thin, white cylinder lay on the seat next to Lance.

'It is. Where he used to spin out on Fast.' Zeb stepped closer and waved a hand in front of Lance's eyes. Lance didn't blink. 'What a gameblur to have! He's completely locked inside himself.'

'He was in the shop when we were there,' Arizona said. 'He already knew Grimble and everything.'

Zeb bent close and stared into Lance's face. Then he

stepped back and looked at the others. 'What should we do?'

'We'd better not touch him,' Arizona said. 'You saw what happened when I touched Grimble. He could be the same.'

Willis agreed. 'And we don't even know if we can get away from this place. We have to leave him.'

Zeb nodded. Lance hadn't budged the whole time they'd stood there.

Willis guessed Zeb's thoughts: this man could be his father.

'C'mon,' Willis whispered. 'We've got to keep looking for a way out.'

As in the earlier room, they found a door in the opposite wall. It could simply lead to yet more gameplay, but having no alternative, they took it. It led into another corridor, but this one without a dead end. Choosing a direction based on impulse rather than reason, they ran down one long passage after another, half-supporting Zeb whenever their hurried pace became too much for him. Finally, they came to a familiar window; it depicted the deep-sea scenario from the Eelements level. But things had changed since Willis and Arizona last saw it. They stared through the window in horror. The young woman drifted lifelessly along the seabed, her carcass alive only with the frenetic wriggling of feeding eels.

Arizona stared as if she couldn't register what she saw, and then she pointed at the controls beneath the window. Though the panel was dull – clearly switched off by someone – the controls had been left in their highest positions. 'Somebody turned it up again.' Her eyes widened with realisation. 'Do you think it's because of us? Because we've got Zeb and we've weakened him? Is this how Grimble gets a new fix?'

Willis grabbed her shoulders and stared into her eyes. 'We are trying to make him weaker and it seems to be working. But he did this, Ari, not us.' He was about to say more but broke off. Arizona had stiffened, looking past him.

She patted him on the sleeve, and indicated a distance behind his shoulder. 'And he's found us,' she said. 'Already.'

'*Found you?*' said a voice.

Willis turned and saw Grimble. As they looked, his face shifted to a smirking Lance and back. He shrugged his shoulders, swinging the rockshocker around, and levelled it at Willis. 'Don't you get that I see exactly where you are *all* the time? After all, this entire place ... it's all me.'

'So what are you going to do with us?' Arizona asked.

Zeb pointed to the gamespace window with the dead woman. 'He doesn't care. As long as he can get us gaming again. His way.'

Arizona leant close to Willis's ear. 'Wouldn't using a real weapon down here be like shooting himself?'

Willis nodded slightly. She was right. If the whole place was Grimble gamespace, created from Zeb's gameblur and those countless Plush gamers – if it was *all me*, as Grimble had said – then firing something he'd brought in from the real world couldn't be a good idea. And what wasn't good for Grimble might be okay for them. It was a risk worth taking – a new strategy. And trying out new strategies was what good gaming was all about. So, how to get him to fire it, but not at them?

He pointed into the deadly Eelements gamespace. 'If we must game somewhere, I want to go here,' he said out loud.

'Me too,' Arizona said, though Willis could detect the confusion in her tone.

Grimble grinned. 'What a coincidence. It just so happens I pushed that one too hard. It's recently become available.'

'Have you both lost your heads?' said Zeb to Willis and Arizona. He looked shocked. 'That's no gamespace I want to visit.' He glanced back into the gamespace scenario. 'Look at her – she's dead! Luckily she's not in Virtualitee. This is just a view into her gamespace, not a room down here in Grimble Land, like I had.'

Willis tensed himself in readiness for Grimble's reaction. Zeb was wrong – he believed the only way into that girl's hellish game was through her bedroom, where her Plush console sat in the real world. But Willis was banking on there being another way, a hazardous way that Grimble would take out of mad impulse – and hopefully pay the price for.

Grimble snorted at Zeb. 'Wrong! I developed the Plush console. Do you think I'm merely viewing their individual gamespaces from the outside? Already I'm sucking off the small amounts of gameblur they're collectively generating. They're my hive of buzzing gamefreaks and I can open any Plush gamespace I like.' He directed the rockshocker at the gamespace window. 'So how about a little gameplay?' The muzzle's snaking wires snapped taut, creating a blinding beam that lit up the gamespace scenario. Grimble pulled the trigger.

Willis threw himself to the floor as a bolt blurted from the rockshocker, shattered the viewing window and embedded in the seabed beyond. Seawater cascaded through the window. The water's chill overwhelmed Willis and he struggled to remain conscious. Kicking off the floor, he rose up and burst to the surface, his head banging on the ceiling. How quickly the corridor filled! He was pressed to the wall and to the side of the window. Far enough away from the direct force of the torrent that gushed through the shattered window.

Twisting about, he could see Arizona directly ahead of him, her hyperboard bobbing up beside her. Then Zeb broke the surface, gasping for air. Unlike Willis, they were dragged to the centre, where the power of the torrent was at its strongest. 'Ari! Zeb!' Willis cried. He watched in horror as they were swept away, disappearing around a bend.

He pushed down deep into the water, staying close to the wall and fighting against the undertow. He could just make out the gamespace control panels further along the corridor. They were spitting sparks and creating an underwater electrical storm. As they exploded outwards, the windows cracked and shattered into the corridor, and the many views into scenarios around the world blanked out.

He twisted in the other direction and saw the wrecked gamespace window. The raging seawater had torn it wider and eaten into the surrounding walls. And he could see Grimble. He seemed unaffected by the force of the water. He stood on the corridor floor. Willis watched as he stepped through the blasted

window and into the Eelements gamespace. Willis rose
to the surface, gasped for air and plunged down again,
determined to see more. When he reached the lethal
fish, Grimble turned and looked directly at Willis. He
raised one arm in his direction. Bubbles burst from
his mouth. Willis knew what he was saying: *Game on.*
The long white fish abandoned the remaining shreds of
the body of the scuba-diving gamer girl, formed a tight
school and shot past Grimble and towards the gaping
window and Willis.

But there was another danger. Grimble, no space
miner, clearly knew nothing of rockshocker mechanics.
The rockshocker bolt was buried somewhere in the
seabed. There was a delay, Willis remembered – which
meant the real blast was yet to come …

The school of fish were pouring into the Virtualitee
gamespace when the blast came. The roar thumped
through Willis and dragged him deeper, spinning and
reeling. The killer fish dropped away, stunned. And
Willis caught one last sight of Grimble. The blast had
erupted from the seabed beneath his feet, but instead
of obliteration, something else happened. It was as if
Grimble had merely been holding on to the image of
a body, and now he let it go. In place of Grimble there
moved a wide, heaving mud-grey shape the consistency
of thick, melting rubber. Willis was looking at pure

gameblur. The rubber stretched until it became a giant eel with white eyes.

Willis burst to the surface, choking as he swallowed air and water. The current dragged him down again. This time he didn't fight it. He let the tunnel of ocean suck him in and hurtle him down the corridor.

CHAPTER 29

Dragged down by the undertow, Willis stretched his body and relaxed. Now and then, he fought for control, rose to the surface and gulped precious air. He tried to reassure himself that even a gamespace ocean emptying itself into subterranean warehouse corridors in a place called Virtualitee had to level off sometime, had to grow calm. And thankfully it did. Eventually the flow subsided and the level dropped.

As Willis bodysurfed in, he spied Arizona and Zeb ahead of him, waist deep in the seawater.

All was quiet about them. The gamespace windows were blank, destroyed by the water. Carcasses of the many slender, vicious fish that had obeyed Grimble's command lapped against the windows' edges and corridor walls.

Zeb and Arizona waded over, Arizona still clutching her hyperboard.

'He's coming,' Willis said. 'We have to keep moving.' He explained what he'd seen. Grimble as pure gameblur. Like an enormous eel.

They took a turning further ahead and waded down corridor after corridor. After a while, they came upon windows that were only now succumbing to the water damage. On either side of them control panels sparked and exploded into the water, severing the connections to Plushes around the world. Gamespaces depicting seedy streets, haunted mansions, vampire lairs, volcanic moonscapes and gore-filled battlefields all suddenly vanished.

Through one window, Willis saw two boys on a high cliff. They were fending off a dragon the colour of dark blood. The dragon's long neck curled and uncurled as it hung in the air, then its head shot forward and blue and white fire disgorged from its nostrils, engulfing them. Dropping to their knees, the boys swung their shields over their heads for protection.

'Remind you of anyone?' said Zeb.

The control panel beneath the window sparked and exploded, and the window blinked off and split apart.

'C'mon, if I found you guys so easily, Grimble can too.'

They pressed ahead at a half-run, trying not to slip in the chilly water. After several more turns they found the water level dropped to below their knees and the gamespace windows were still intact. The sound of exploding panels was a distant echo, though it was difficult to say from which direction it came. Willis glanced at Arizona and caught her watching him. She smiled and he smiled back.

'This Virtualitee is enormous,' she said. She spoke in frustration but there was also a sense of wonder in her voice.

'Gamespace is as big as it needs to be,' Zeb called from a short distance behind them. 'At least the water's levelling off.' Since meeting up again, he'd managed to walk unaided, but now he stopped and leant against the nearest gamespace window. His face paled as he turned and glanced through it. 'Oh no,' he said. 'I don't believe it.'

Willis and Arizona waded back and looked.

There, in the gamespace, in bright orange bathers, was Ms Loveland. She sat at a patio table.

'The *EleMental* version of the Floating Baths,' Zeb said.

Willis gazed at the scene. 'It's still on. In my bed-room.'

Zeb turned from the view. 'Let's get away from here.'

Willis shook his head and indicated the window. 'No, Zeb. We've found our way out. That's my Plush. I am the Plush owner. I command it.' At least I hope so, Willis thought, wishing he felt as confident as he sounded.

They stared at him, puzzled. Then Zeb's eyes widened. 'That's a rough game in there. And what if Grimble, monster eel or otherwise, yanks up the dials to the lethal level?'

Arizona looked like she was about to agree, but suddenly turned away – something else had caught her attention. Willis was about to ask what when he noticed something too. He looked down. The water.

Arizona pointed back up the corridor. 'What's that? Not Grimble, but ...'

Willis only half took in her words. 'This water hasn't levelled off at all. It's rising.' It licked at his thighs, creeping higher. And he realised the sound of exploding panels was once more within earshot – and coming closer.

He pointed to the window again. 'This has to be our way out of here. We'll have to be quick though. Grimble won't be able to yank the dials once the panel's destroyed by water. But we need to find a way in before the screen cuts out.'

The water was almost up to his waist. He could hear the explosions creep steadily closer. Window after window blanked out, shattered and fell into the water.

'I mean it, guys,' Arizona said louder. 'I saw—'

The underwater movement of a dense, curling line caught Willis's eye. Then the water before them erupted as a massive eel reared up.

Willis turned to Arizona. 'Quick! Your hyperboard.' He jabbed a finger at the window.

Arizona held the hyperboard's erupter above the water and thumped at it with her fist. It failed to start. She tried again without success.

'It's too wet!'

'Keep trying!' Willis urged, still transfixed by the new Grimble eel.

It emitted a hollow groan, like wind through a tunnel. And then from its thickness a head forced itself into shape. Ms Loveland's face was looking at Willis.

'Still gameplaying after what we agreed?' it shrieked. 'You'll never come to anything.' Willis's mother's head appeared to one side. 'Don't blame him,' it said. 'He's a good boy, really. Just a bit of a loner, like his dad. He finds it hard to make friends.' Zeb's mother's face appeared below Willis's mother's. 'All this gameplay can't be good for your mental health,' it said. 'At the very least, it should be limited to weekends and term breaks.' A long arm splurted from the eel's surface, clutching an enormous wineglass. Zeb's mother's face smacked its lips and guzzled from it. Then Lance's muscular shoulders and face ripped from one side of the eel's trunk. 'Gaming's too schoffin' violent,' it growled. Other faces came and went in a continuous flow, all spitting advice. Even the face of Todd pushed through next to Ms Loveland's. 'Losers,' it sneered. And, of course, Grimble was in there too, his grey face and black sunglasses coming and going. He scowled at Willis. 'There's no way out of here, Willis Jaxon. There's only gaming. Forever and ever and ever.'

Behind him, Willis could hear Arizona's attempts to start her hyperboard and her cries of frustration. 'I don't mean to pressure you, Ari,' he called over his shoulder, 'but hurry up!'

'I'm trying, I'm trying!'

All of the heads were sucked – *schlop* – back into the eel, and Grimble's head, arms and torso ripped into being from its upper half. 'Would you like to know the score?'

'No thanks,' said Willis.

Two arms grew from Grimble and he lurched at Willis. And past him. It seemed that Zeb, standing to one side and silently gawping at the whole scene, was Grimble's real target.

'Hey!' Zeb yelled, twisting in Grimble's arms.

Grimble drew him in close. 'Come to me, Zeb Redman.'

Willis thrust one hand into Grimble's face, his left cheek. But it didn't have the desired effect, the Arizona effect. Instead of Willis's hand pushing through to the other side it melted into Grimble, increasing the mass of his head. Willis wrenched it out and gaped at it. It was fingerless! And it was fuzzy, out of focus. He could *feel* his fingers but couldn't see them. He spread the feeling of his fingers wide. Slowly, with a slurp, they re-emerged from the centre of his hand and sharpened into focus.

Still gripping Zeb, Grimble smiled.

'Hurry, Ari,' Willis said again. 'I think he's trying to kick in Zeb's gameblur. We could all be swallowed up in it.'

'Oh, I think I'm beyond all that, don't you?' Grimble said. 'I've got you all hooked, lined and sinkered.'

The windows on either side of the corridor two down from them blanked out. A second later, in unison, the control panels blasted outwards.

'Ari, we're about to lose our window!'

Grimble's face dissolved into the smooth greyness of the eel once more, and the water around Zeb disappeared. Somehow he stood on dry land, dressed in a gleaming battle uniform. A shining silver needle-gun swung from his shoulder.

'Zeb,' Willis hollered. 'Gameblur! Shut it down.'

'Game on,' Zeb said. He stepped into the eel and the eel lurched, growing higher, doubling in size.

The window next to the Floating Baths gamespace broke off, sparking and shattering.

A new arm shot from the Grimble eel and grabbed Willis. It dragged him towards it. Arizona shoved past him, swinging her hyperboard – a blur of crimson – over her head.

'Take *this*!'

Her hyperboard slammed into the main mass of the eel. The end that housed the board's small erupter sunk in. Willis heard the hyperboard's erupter kick into life. Though muffled, there was no doubting its distinct *thrum*.

The eel jolted into a rigid posture. Falling backwards, it released Willis's arm and spewed out a dazed Zeb. Then the hyperboard itself burst from the eel, its suspension lasers blazing and its erupter bucking with energy. Arizona fought to hang onto it. Stunned, the Grimble eel sunk beneath the water. Arizona plunged her shuddering hyperboard deep into the water and bounded on, revving it full tilt to keep the erupter from flooding with seawater.

Willis watched amazed as she soared into the air atop the hyperboard. She spun over the water in a twenty-one-sixty popshoveit – the name her virtual self had given it, Willis remembered – then threw herself off as the hyperboard crashed into the Floating Baths window, smashing it.

Willis recovered faster than Zeb, who no longer wore battle armour and was bent over in concentration. Working at controlling his gameblur, Willis guessed. The water now licked at the gamespace control panel, seeping into it. Willis knew it was about to explode, unjacking the Floating Baths gamespace from where they stood. He shoved Zeb towards the demolished window. They were just behind Arizona, who was already clambering across the window's threshold and preparing to leap into the gamespace beyond. The control panel ruptured into sparks as Willis and Zeb threw themselves across, almost crushing Arizona beneath them as they tumbled into the gamespace.

Willis rolled head over heels in warmer water and broke to the surface to discover he now swam in the groundwater lanes he'd always favoured. The intense, steamy atmosphere caused him to gasp after the icy seawater. Arizona trod water near him. Zeb spluttered and thrashed, barely keeping his head above surface. Willis forced them to keep moving. He and Arizona pushed towards the shallow end, Zeb once more supported by their arms.

When they'd first sighted Ms Loveland from within Virtualitee, she'd been on the far side at a patio table. Now she ran to the edge of the water and dived in. Willis could see her change as she streaked through the water, becoming grey and elongated. Others joined her, the virtual Todd, Arizona, himself. His parents. All slick-skinned and eel-like.

There was a small explosion. Willis glanced back in its direction. He knew it had to be the panel – the connection with Virtualitee was broken. To his horror, he saw something else in the water, something mud-grey and thick.

They were under attack from both sides.

'Attention, Plush,' Willis called. 'Can you hear me, Plush?'

'Plush here,' said the polite female Plush voice.

Willis sucked in a deep breath to shout his next words but drew only water deep into his lungs as he was yanked beneath the surface. Something gripped his ankles and hauled him backwards through the groundwater lanes. A bloated, nauseating pain ripped through his guts and he convulsed, spewing and sucking in water. Creatures with familiar yet unfamiliar faces – evil parodies of people he knew – shrieked in delight around him. Willis reached back and clawed at the fingers that gripped his ankles. And then he flew from the water, rising feet-first high into the air. The other creatures stayed alongside him, swirling and gleeful. When he stopped, hanging like a carcass on a meat hook, he knew where he must be: the Bubble Arena. He attempted to cry out to the Plush again but only gagged on more water as it erupted from his chest, coursing through his throat and nose.

As if the creature read his intention, he was on the move again, unable to speak. The other creatures jabbered with joy as he was dragged backwards, smashing through one giant floating glob of water after another.

Below, Arizona and Zeb stared up in terror. They splashed through the shallow end of the groundwater lanes, creatures at their ankles. Further behind, extending high out of the water but motionless and watching, as if overseeing all the proceedings, was the Grimble eel.

Willis clawed uselessly at the fingers that locked about his ankles, then looked into the eyes of the creature that held him captive. It was himself: his evil, virtual self.

It snickered then bared its mouth of needle-teeth, clearly pleased to be recognised.

Willis drew in a harsh breath, relieved to fill his lungs with air. 'I know what's happening here. Grimble's *still* trying to get us to play his game. But if I do, I'll have lost. So I won't fight you.'

The creature snarled.

'Well,' Willis added as if in afterthought, 'maybe just a little.' He smashed the creature in the face with all his might. Then he flopped back down.

'Plush!' Willis yelled while he still had a chance.

'Still here,' said the Plush. Calm. Neutral.

'This is Willis Jaxon. Shut down this game.' There was a brief moment of silence. Willis added: 'Please.'

'Shutting down game,' said the Plush voice. It almost sounded cheerful. Oblivious.

'Thank you,' Willis croaked.

'You're welcome. You are very polite.'

The gamespace began to break up at the seams. Beneath the gamespace, Willis could detect the outlines of his beautiful, wonderful, longed-for, dirty-white bedroom walls. And he felt the grip on his ankles loosen. He glanced up in time to see the virtual version of himself stretch. Then it was whipped into the beginnings of the folding. Willis's bed materialised just in time for him to fall onto it. He bounced off the mattress, ran over and flattened himself against his bedroom wall. His *real* wall in his *real* bedroom. Turning, he pressed his back to the wall and watched as the gamespace was gathered into the folding: the small yellow bridge, the surrounding walkways, the patio with its tables and chairs, the great globs of high, floating water, all sucked in.

He spotted the outline of the virtual Ms Loveland. The creature swam fast, but could not escape the Plush's folding. It whipped the creature up, groundwater lane and all, and sent it spinning into a blur within its vortex.

But one thing resisted, rising from the groundwater lanes as they were sucked into the folding. It was the Grimble eel – pure gameblur shaped loosely as the long, grey creature. It did something Willis hadn't thought possible: it extended itself until two thirds of its massive length hung beyond the folding parameters and into Willis's realspace bedroom. It faced Willis, white pupils unblinking, impervious to the chaos of the folding game about it.

Willis froze under the creature's steel gaze.

Then it pulled back. A cobra about to strike.

Willis gulped in fear.

'Willis!' Arizona's urgent cry fired him into action. With his shoulders pressed to the wall, he lashed out with his right leg. His foot connected with the Grimble eel's head and smacked it to one side. He did no real damage, but Willis saw the surprise in its white eyes – and then the sudden realisation it had lost its moment.

The folding engulfed it and dragged it into its dense tornado.

As the grey mass spun into a blur, Grimble's old face, complete with black, impenetrable sunglasses, emerged from the maelstrom. '*Noooo*,' came his cry from the blurred mess of spinning shapes and colours. '*Noooo!*'

The folding thickened into one blinding spot of light.

Pop.

Willis looked across the room at Zeb and Arizona. Like him, they stood with their backs to the bedroom wall. No one moved.

An early morning light streamed through the bedroom window. Precious reality hung all about them. Willis sucked in cool air, filling his lungs with it. He stretched his arms wide into the rays of sunlight and spread his fingers.

His movement shook the others from their stillness. They moved together towards the centre of the room and leant in, holding each other.

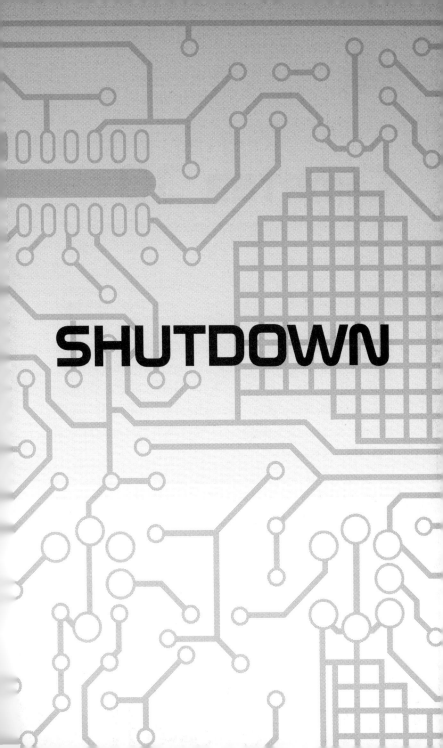

SHUTDOWN

CHAPTER 30

Willis carried his Plush under one arm and held Arizona's hand.

The keen spring wind that seemed to blow in all directions at once stung his face with dirt. It felt authentic. It had its task: shake the seeds from their homes and scatter them in readiness for the city's well-known bursts of spring rain followed by splashes of sun. Real-world stuff.

Willis shivered at the memory of Virtualitee. He let go of Arizona's hand and pointed. 'This is it, I think. According to Zeb's directions.'

They stood at a plain door. To the door's right, metal sheeting hung over what used to be a store window.

'They're living in a disused milk bar?' Arizona said.

A tall man answered the door when they buzzed. He had the look of someone who'd been spacefronting:

the bloodless, pasty face. The stoop. But he also had a special energy. Like Zeb. It lived in his eyes. When he smiled at them, Willis couldn't help but beam back. His smile was like Zeb's: winning.

Could this man be Zeb's father? Willis wondered. It was possible. They shared traits. Yet Zeb also shared one very significant trait with Lance – a susceptibility to gameblur.

'Mr Redman?'

The man nodded. 'It's Willis, isn't it? I've heard about you from Zeb. And Arizona, hello.' He gave a quizzical glance in the direction of the Plush under Willis's arm.

'This is one of those Plush consoles,' Willis explained. 'It's not working properly.'

Zeb's father nodded again, in a thoughtful way. 'Faulty consoles have been around as long as gaming itself. Some kind of gremlin?'

'More a fish, really.'

Arizona chuckled.

Mr Redman blinked back at them, obviously confused. 'Well, I hope you get a replacement. One without any kind of resident.'

'Thank you. Meanwhile, there's still something we need to do. And we thought Zeb might want to be a part of it.'

'Well, wait here – we've only moved in and everything's a mess.' He turned to go then turned back. 'My son's been less than forthcoming with details about when he went missing.' He sighed and shook his head. 'Long may that Lance Hack remain missing. But Zeb tells me he couldn't have got through it – whatever *it* is – without your help. Thank you. You're good friends.'

After he left, Arizona indicated the Plush. 'Are you sure he's in there?'

Willis gave a small shrug.

Zeb was only a moment and was clearly dressed to go out.

'Leave the hyperboard,' Willis said. 'We're only going down to the junction.'

Zeb agreed without asking for an explanation.

'I haven't dared eject the game or anything,' Willis said as they headed off. 'I've just made sure it can't accidentally power up.' He turned the Plush around and showed them. Where the minute zippatronic configurations used to be there was a hole and a mass of jagged cracks.

'Whoa.' Zeb shook his head in admiration. 'How'd you do that?'

'With a brick.'

Zeb looked stunned. Arizona laughed.

* * *

They stood at the security rail beyond a sharp bend and before the ziptram junction with its series of platforms. They didn't have to wait long before they heard the approaching tram. From the direction of the sound, they could tell it came up from the city. Perfect. The air filled with the screams and rattling of its heavy engines. It was one of the big ones.

It lurched into view as it sped towards the bend before the junction. A double-decker. It sucked dirt and dust into a small tornado beneath it. Its side panels sported a zipanimated ad for an upcoming sunsurfer event. The moving graphic – a long solar flare with coiling, crimson flames – covered the vehicle's whole length.

'Maybe this isn't such a good idea,' Arizona said.

'I'll be right back.' Willis dragged his gaze from the tram and pushed himself up onto the security rail. He threw the Plush over first and then clambered after it. He now stood in illegal territory and felt sure that in a room somewhere an alarm was screaming. He had thirty seconds if he was lucky.

Behind him, the ziptram continued to rise. He tried not to think about what he was doing, the madness of it. Both he and the roaring vehicle made for the same scrap of ground.

In order to negotiate the bend, ziptrams had to rise nose first far above the ground, twist, then plunge to the junction and tram stop immediately after it. This was the highest and fastest ziptram dumpdown Willis knew.

He glanced up at the tram; it had reached the zenith of its turn and angled over the zipcars that buzzed on the intersection beneath it.

It tilted. It turned. It was coming in.

Willis measured out an imaginary line from the direction of the tram's nose to the ground, then threw the Plush to the ground a short distance before him. The console landed with a thud – but not where he'd intended. Though already running away, he checked himself. No point in doing this and doing it wrong. He ran back to the console and kicked it into better position. Then he paused.

Was that his imagination or could he hear something? Cries?

'Noo! Noo!'

Zeb and Arizona called to him from where they hid in a dilapidated wooden tram shelter.

At their beckoning, Willis looked up and found himself peering directly into the face of the descending tram. It roared towards him, its steel wheels emerging, positioning. He was so close he could see directly into the cockpit. The trampilot looked horrified. Willis couldn't hear him, but he could see him shouting and gesticulating. Willis turned and bolted. As he ran, the shadow of the fiery ziptram raced along the ground behind him, like a giant predator in a virtual game. The rapid gunfire clanging of the tram's bell, overworked by the trampilot, spurred Willis on until he threw himself over the rail and into the mud on the other side.

Hunched against the rail, he watched as the ziptram dumped to the ground, pulverising the Plush into the earth. There was a long scream as the tram came to a halt and the doors opened. Commuters spilled out.

'C'mon,' Willis called. Being a large junction the tram stop was graced with a series of platforms. Willis ran along the rail until he reached the platform the ziptram had glided alongside. The ziptram's entrance remained open, waiting, and he clambered up the three steps. He didn't bother to look back; he knew Zeb and Ari were close behind.

For a laugh, they didn't use the seats and strapped themselves into the economy harnesses. Arizona grabbed at a safety bar and swung herself up, her harness straining. She kicked Willis in the stomach. 'Hey! I'm a ninja!'

'No you're not. You're a-nnoying.' He rubbed his stomach as if it were sore.

Zeb smiled at Willis. 'Never thought I'd see you like this.'

'I'm amazed you're still talking to me after what I just did.'

'To your old Plush?' He laughed. 'Forget about it. Haven't you heard? A brand-zoomin-new console's coming out. The Plush Plus. I'm aching for it.'

They turned in their harnesses and peered through the window at the street scene that sped past. The long line of cafes with customers at outdoor tables, the window displays, the shoppers with money to burn, the hawkers with their handicrafts on street trolleys, the buskers, the pavement chalk painters, the buzzing zipcars that jostled for position beneath the tram …

Willis squinted and let it all blur before his eyes. 'It's all going on out there, isn't it?' he said.

'Score,' said a voice in the air.

Willis spun around.

It was Zeb. Looking at him. Grinning.

ΛCKNOWLEDGMENTS

I am grateful to Varuna – The Writers' House and the Eleanor Dark Foundation for their support, in particular Mark Macleod, Varuna young adult fiction mentor, and Peter Bishop, Creative Director.

I also owe special thanks to Gina Woodhead, my wife, for her encouragement and patience; Dexy Woodhead for his incisive videogame advice; Mairead Acushla O'Connor for her unwavering support; Lily O'Shea (my mother) and Lisa Reece-Lane, my energetic writing buddies who share my love of writing; my other family members and friends Debra O'Connor, Ursula O'Connor, Bryan O'Connor, David O'Connor, Carol O'Connor, Sparks Woodhead, Chris Sarandis, Rino Lalli, Jayashri Kulkarni, Ernie Butler, Robyn Ramsden, Jude Quinn and Rosa Billi for their enthusiasm and interest; Jack Schlueter and Dexy (again) for their skateboarding tips; my fellow Varuna writers, Kylie Stevenson, Gillian M Wadds, Ian Trevaskis, Nicole Hayes and Meg McKinlay; past great supporters, Rachel Flynn, Janey Runci and Anne Brown; and finally Colette Vella, publisher, and Ali Lavau, editor – for liking my story about Willis, Arizona and Zeb, and for their incredible final production efforts – and all the team at Pier 9.